W9-CPA-800

The Hong Bay district of Hong Kong
is fictitious, as are the people who,
for one reason or another, inhabit it.

SCI FI

A YELLOWTHREAD STREET MYSTERY

William Marshall

An Owl Book

HOLT, RINEHART AND WINSTON
New York

Copyright © 1981 by William Marshall
All rights reserved, including the right to reproduce this
book or portions thereof in any form.
Published by Holt, Rinehart and Winston,
383 Madison Avenue, New York, New York 10017.

Library of Congress Cataloging in Publication Data
Marshall, William Leonard, 1944-
Sci fi: a Yellowthread Street mystery.
I. Title.
PR9619.3.M275S3   1981   823   80-27264
ISBN 0-03-071063-4 (An Owl bk.) (pbk.)

First published in hardcover by Holt, Rinehart and Winston
in 1981.

First Owl Book Edition—1984

Printed in the United States of America
1 3 5 7 9 10 8 6 4 2

ISBN 0-03-071063-4

1

The Martians had landed.

And, with them, the Venusians, the Saturnians, the Moon-People, Gill-Man, the entire complement of Star Wars extra-terrestrials, Chest-burster, Batman, Superman, Spiderman, The Hulk, The Alien, The Contagion, and, for the joy of antique and nostalgic older souls, several variations of Oriental Bela Lugosi, Lon Chaney, Boris Karloff and – particularly popular among the more diminutive – Peter Lorre and The Incredible Shrinking Man.

The second day of the All-Asia Science Fiction and Horror Movie Congress was in full swing in Hong Bay and so far there had been so many outside invasions of the place by sea and by land that if Paul Revere had been resurrected to take on the task of announcing them to the Colonials he would have retired from the scene with terminal laryngitis after the first fifteen aircraft-fuls.

To date, in the midst of cheering crowds of never less than five thousand dressed-up raving and cheering fans, the publicity men had:

(a) launched a helium-filled Death Star from the roof of the six storey Empress of India hotel in the general direction of Indonesia, Australia and the Antarctic – fortunately for world peace shot down by an aghast A. A. battery just as it crossed immediately and provocatively across the border into Red China—

(b) christened with a massed shriek of delight the

1

maiden voyage of the Thing From Beneath The Sea – The Thing, an enormous hairy sausage some sixty foot long had instantly snagged the propellers of a freighter loaded with high explosives and been untangled and sunk without trace by a slightly anxious Water Police –

(c) tried, for some totally mysterious and unthinkable purpose, to land a massed bank of tungsten-steel cutting lasers which were, happily for the continuance of civilisation as we knew it, confiscated at the airport by a small army of terrified and trembling wild-eyed Customs officers ...

Meanwhile the ledge hanging abilities of The Human Fly at 5 a.m. had thrilled hundreds. A lecher bent on the defloration of a less than willing young lady on the eighth floor of a block of government housing apartments, his screams for help as she shut her open window suddenly on his fingers had roused thousands.

A small riot had been narrowly averted when Space Warrior, armed with his sword and his mission to make the Galaxy a safe place to live in, had decided to take on a few Chinese rowdies in Icehouse Street and discovered that, as well as not being fans of Space Warrior, the rowdies were in fact a peaceful group of kung-fu enthusiasts celebrating the promotion of one of their number to Black Belt status.

A group of very drunken World Killers bent on finding a world to kill ...

*

In the Detectives' Room, Senior Detective Inspector Christopher O'Yee shrieked, 'I'm running out of space!' It had reached the point where he had a schematic of the cells spread out on his desk like the cabin plan to the Queen Mary. He counted the cells for the eighth time in ten minutes and still came up with the same statistics: fourteen cells and sixteen prisoners not counting The

Green Slime in cell twelve and something of indeterminate sexual persuasion calling itself The Object in cell eight, two Godzillas in eleven, The Human Fly in six, in cell seven—. He looked down at the schematic for steerage. The only steerage was a broom cupboard. There were a series of grunts outside as Constable Yan struggled with God knew what fresh in from the streets, and O'Yee yelled out through the open door, 'Is it male or female?'

There were more grunts and then Yan's voice yelled back, a moment before someone hit him, 'How do I know? It looks like a cross between Wonder Woman and The Incredible Hulk! Where do I put it?'

'Put it with The Object in cell eight!' There was a fire point near the broom cupboard with, fortunately, a lockable door. It might be handy if they got in any midgets. That was, if the fire hose once The Object and Yan's catch got together, wasn't needed for more urgent things. O'Yee demanded, 'Why the hell don't you stop bringing these people in?'

Yan went, 'Oof!' as another blow struck him and gave a grunt as he drew his baton and struck back. Yan called back, 'They're all criminals, sir—obviously.' He added as an afterthought, 'Ow!'

'But I'm running out of space!'

'Get North Point Station to take some.'

'North Point ran out of cells four hours ago. North Point have got The Swarm.'

Yan complained, 'I missed that one!' He was referring not to the movie, but to a point on Hulk/Wonderwoman's anatomy. He rectified the omission with a blow of his baton that terminated with a thud as Hulk/Wonderwoman made a nose dive for the floor. Yan trumpeted, 'Got you, you—'

O'Yee consulted his cabin plan and tried to correlate it with a sheaf of arrest reports. 'Yan, did you arrest The Green Slime?'

3

'Me, sir? No. Why?'

'Because I haven't got an arrest form for him!' O'Yee thought of going out into the charge room in order to stop shouting, decided that the last thing he felt like doing in a morass of forms was filling out a Witness To Brutality Statement, 'I can't find an arrest report for him anywhere!' He called out, 'Constable Sun, are you there?'

He wasn't.

'Constable Lee, did you arrest The Green Slime and forget to make out an arrest form?'

A voice called out, 'Give me a hand!' and there was a fresh series of oofs and grunts as Lee evidently joined in the morning's sport of Hulk/Wonderwoman whacking. Lee yelled out, 'No, sir, not me.'

Auden and Spencer had been at the Canton Road carpark since 4 a.m. It couldn't have been them. O'Yee appealed, 'Do you know if Mr Feiffer—' He got no reply, 'Do you know if anyone in the goddamned place has bothered to—' O'Yee yelled at the top of his voice, *'Constable Sun, where the hell are you?'* His phone rang and he snatched it up.

It was the duty officer at North Point mentioning politely that the paddy wagon had picked up thirty or forty drunks dressed identically as The Thing From Beyond Space, and, speaking of space—

O'Yee said, 'No! Forget it! Try goddamned Wan Chai Station!'

'Wan Chai Station is full of hookers and pimps—'

'Then Yaumati over on—'

The duty officer at North Point said, 'A gang of mad Australians wearing Ned Kelly helmets and carrying space boomerangs. I think it's a character from some obscene Antipodean comic strip called Iron Outlaw or—'

'Kai Tak?'

'Amok Malaysians wielding—'

'Juvenile?'

'Do you mean have we got any spare juveniles in our cells or has Juvenile got any spare cells? Yes, we've got some spare juveniles – about twenty to be precise – and no, Juvenile hasn't got any spare cells.' The duty officer paused for a moment, 'Either that or they're midgets.' He asked, 'Why? Could you take a few midgets or something?'

'No, we couldn't take a few midgets or something! What do you think your goddamned fire hose cupboard is for?'

'Our fire hose cupboard was smashed to bits yesterday afternoon by Wolf Man and The Adder People.' The duty officer at North Point said, 'Hey, Christopher, I don't want to sound like I'm whining for a favour or anything, and I wouldn't actually like to come right out and say that any little assistance you could give me might be more than amply repaid in the future—'

O'Yee said with a snarl, 'Good, then don't say it!' He asked, 'Listen, The Green Slime, by any chance did you—'

Yan yelled out, 'Constable Sun, there's another one outside, pissing in public—' and O'Yee yelled out, 'Don't bother, we don't want him!' a moment before the duty officer at North Point bellowed in his ear, 'Don't send him to us!'

'I wasn't going to!'

Sun said, 'I'll get him!'

'It's not a him!'

Sun said, dropping his voice, interested, 'Really?'

O'Yee tried hopelessly, 'Sun! The Green Slime—'

The North Point duty officer shouted down the line, 'No! No!' He roared at someone in his own station, 'Don't just stand there! Hit him!'

O'Yee hung up.

The Hulk/Wonderwoman yelled out ominously (metamorphosising?), 'RAA—YAGH!'

'Sun!'

Nothing.

O'Yee looked down at the cabin plan and, sticking his

fingers in his ears, wondered if ever on the old Queen Mary the purser, finally driven out of his goddamned mind, had gone downstairs, caught half a dozen of the passengers by the ears, and then bodily thrown them overboard. He snapped out as Detective Chief Inspector Harry Feiffer came in through the door carrying two cups of coffee, 'Harry! Where the hell have you been?'

Feiffer looked surprised. 'In bed. I'm not on until 6.' Outside in the corridor, Sun, evidently having failed to find his more interesting quarry, had dragged in someone dressed as a Chinese Batman. The someone dressed as a Chinese Batman had his hands around Sun's throat and was in the process of determining by scientific method how hard he had to press before Sun's face, going purple, went to the full end of the colour spectrum at black. Sun called out, 'Yan! Lee!'

Feiffer said, 'Why? What's the problem?'

'I'm running out of cells. The problem is that those idiots out there have gone mad arresting people and I haven't got anywhere to put them! The problem is—*the problem is that The Green Slime hasn't even got an arrest sheet!*'

Feiffer said, 'Oh.' Sun, by the simple technique of near collapse had got Batman down onto the floor and was in the process of removing his fingers from his neck and seeing how far back he could bend them against Batman's wrists before his eyes popped out. Batman made a series of rumbling noises and tried to land a kick in Sun's nether regions. Sun avoided the kick and bashed Batman's bat ears against the ground.

Feiffer said innocently, 'Never heard of him. It wasn't me.' He looked down at the moving battle on the floor and asked Sun, 'Do you want a hand?'

Sun already had two of them, both belonging to Batman. He twisted them around the Caped Crusader's cowl, got an encouraging death rattle started, and, getting to his feet like a wrestler, kneed Batman in the utility belt.

Sun said, 'No, thanks. It's a Uniform Branch matter really, sir.'

Batman shrilled out, 'How the hell was I to know he was straight? It's common knowledge Robin is gay! What the hell does he get up to all day in the goddamned Bat Cave if he doesn't—'

Sun brought his knee up again, missed, and as Batman got a damaged gloved paw loose and inserted a finger in his eye, fell over, reaching for his truncheon.

O'Yee said, *'I haven't got a cell!'* His protest was lost as Batman snaked his hand out to grab Sun around the ankles and screamed, 'I'm going to kill you you brutal butch bastard!' His mouth changed into a round O as Feiffer set the two cups of coffee on a filing cabinet by the door and stood on his fingers.

O'Yee said to the cabin plan as the message from Feiffer's heel got through in a flash to Batman's tonsils and Batman began screaming, 'There's just no organisation in the place! No organisation at all!' His phone rang again and O'Yee snarled out, 'No, we can't take them whatever they are! We've got every goddamned maniac, pervert, flasher, jerk-off artist, retcher, midget, mugger and god-damned sonofabitching lunatic we want, so just screw off and find your own goddamned motherloving cell in your own goddamned lousy—'

At the other end of the line his wife said, 'Christopher! What if this had been one of the children ringing up to talk to you?'

From down in the cells, Constable Lee yelled out, 'Sun, are you there? I need help!'

Sun called back, 'I'm bringing Batman down!' Batman, staring at his hand under Feiffer's heel, had a glazed look in his eyes. Sun nodded to Feiffer and said politely, 'Um, thanks, that's fine now—' He called over to O'Yee, 'Sir, where will I put him?'

Emily O'Yee demanded, 'What would the children have

thought? What would Patrick have thought?' She changed her tone to one of pure female menace, 'Or Penelope? *Or little Mary?* Or—'

Sun called out, 'Sir? Mr O'Yee? Where shall I put him?'

'How the fuck do I know where you should put him?' O'Yee, remembering the phone in his hand, said, 'Oh—!'

Feiffer said to Sun, 'Did he actually touch anyone?'

'No, sir. He just offered to touch someone.'

'Where's the complainant?'

'He took off. He said he was going to link up with the end of the Star Wars Two parade in General Gordon Street—'

O'Yee said into the phone, 'I'm sorry, dear. Gosh, I'm really sorry.' He stared around the room desperately, 'Gee whiz, I'm really—'

Feiffer said to Sun, 'There isn't much room in the cells. If the complainant isn't going to complain you may as well chuck him out onto the street again.' He took his heel off Batman's hand and for a moment thought Batman was going to grab his shoe and kiss it.

Batman said in Cantonese, 'May all the heavens bless you, sir!' He said, 'Ugh!' as Sun decided he was going to get one good retributive kick in before he threw him back.

O'Yee said, 'It's just that, dear ... '

Emily O'Yee, working herself up, said, 'I wasn't going to mention this before, Christopher, but *are you aware you went out this morning and left the front door totally and completely unlocked?*'

'I'm really sorry, dear ... '

Emily said, 'What if Patrick or Penelope or *little Mary* had—'

Feiffer shut the door after Sun and Batman and came forward with the coffee. Feiffer said with a wink, 'Organisation.'

O'Yee said, 'Yes, dear, no dear ... ' He said weakly to Feiffer, 'Tell me about it.'

8

'*Are you trying to be funny?*'

'No, dear! No!'

From the cells, one of the prisoners shrieked out at the top of his lungs, 'Dirty, second-rate, low life, rotten cop *CRUD!*' and O'Yee, gazing up at the ceiling with the coffee from the cup dripping onto his Queen Mary cabin plans, couldn't have agreed more.

*

In the cleared employees' carpark of the Empress of India hotel – the venue for the Congress – there was an eighty foot diameter plywood flying saucer, decal-less, grey-painted, and other-worldly with a fibreglass spaceman on guard by it.

The Star Wars Two parade was in progress out of earshot on the other side of Hong Bay and except for The Spaceman and two T-shirt and shorts clad Chinese street sweepers brushing unhurriedly at the gutters with their wire brooms, the area was still and deserted.

The Spaceman, a life-sized figure in a silver suit and black visored helmet stood a few feet from the saucer like Gort the robot from *The Day The Earth Stood Still*. He had an imitation ray gun of some sort in his silver gloved hand and with the slight wind blowing in from the sea and making creaking noises in the glued joints and plates of the saucer, the ray gun wavered slightly as if the hand holding it might be of frail flesh and blood rather than, like the other statues of Godzilla, Buck Rodgers, Walrus Man et al littering the Hong Bay streets, nothing but locally made moulded fibreglass.

The first sweeper stopping to scratch, waited while his colleague, an older toothless man, wandered up to scratch alongside him, then, leaning on his broom, asked critically, 'Do you think that's any good?'

The second sweeper made a sniffing noise. By the control

dome on the saucer you could see a black stencilled mark. The second sweeper shook his head. The second sweeper said dismissively, 'Nah, that's made out of old tea chests. You can see the black marks they put on tea chests.' He looked at The Spaceman.

There was the faintest clicking sound from The Spaceman's gun.

The first sweeper said thoughtfully, 'Yeah. Unless it's supposed to be a Chinese character?' Like his colleague, he was illiterate. He asked, 'Do you think that's what it is?'

The second sweeper shook his head and felt his gums. The second sweeper said, 'Nah, Martians wouldn't have a Chinese character on their flying saucer, they'd have a Martian character.' He looked up at the mark, 'That looks like Chinese to me.'

The first sweeper had a faint stubble under his chin. He scratched at it with determination. 'Me too.' He turned his attention to The Spaceman, 'Is he supposed to be an Earthman?' The first sweeper said, 'He hasn't got anything written on his suit so he isn't supposed to be Chinese.' He thought about it for a moment, 'If he was supposed to be a Chinese spaceman he'd have a red star or something on his chest, wouldn't he? Unless he's supposed to be a Hong Kong spaceman?'

The second sweeper said, 'Hong Kong hasn't got any spacemen. That's only the Americans and the Russians.'

The click came again from the ray gun, and then, slowly, inexorably The Spaceman's arm moved and the gun came up, swivelled slightly and trained itself on the flying saucer.

The first sweeper said, 'That's good. How do they do that?'

The second sweeper said, 'It's a machine.'

'Yeah.'

The second sweeper said, 'Just so long as they don't make a mess, that's all I care about. You see one of these science fiction movies and they blow down half the

10

city—but do you ever see the poor sods of sweepers cleaning up after them? Nah.' There was a hissing sound coming from the muzzle of the ray gun and then, a fraction of a second later, a fine mist of something filled the air and made the second sweeper gag. The second sweeper said, 'What the hell is—'

The Spaceman, his hand firmly on the butt of the ray gun, turned slightly and placed himself in direct line with the flying saucer. He pressed the trigger.

The flying saucer disappeared into a single ball of roaring, blossoming flame.

There were forty five million dollars involved, minimum. The Spaceman, oblivious to the shouts and protests of the street sweepers, moved on to Stage Two in order to get it.

Raising the ray gun for the second time, he swung it past the blazing, collapsing saucer and, centring the nozzle squarely on the chest of the second sweeper, pressed the trigger and, in a raging stream of pulsing yellow fire, cremated him where he stood.

*

Hong Kong is an island of some 30 square miles under British administration in the South China Sea facing the Kowloon and New Territories areas of continental China. Kowloon and the New Territories are also British administered, surrounded by the Communist Chinese province of Kwangtung. The climate is generally sub-tropical, with hot, humid summers and heavy rainfall. The population of Hong Kong and the surrounding areas at any one time, including tourists and visitors, is in excess of four millions. The New Territories are leased from the Chinese. The lease is due to expire in 1997, but the British nevertheless maintain a military presence along the border, although, should the Communists who supply almost all the Colony's drinking water, ever desire to terminate the lease early, they need only turn off the taps. Hong Bay

11

*is on the southern side of the island and the tourist brochures advise
you not to go there after dark.*

*

7.10 a.m. Monday morning.
At first, people woken from their sleep thought the pall
of smoke could have come from nothing less than a
fully-laden aircraft crashing in the middle of the city.

2

The Government Medical Officer, Doctor Macarthur, lighting a pungent French cigarette from the butt of another only half smoked, touched at the INVASION OF THE BODY SNATCHERS badge on his coat, glanced down at the charred broom and bitumen showing where the street sweeper had died, and said softly, 'I always wanted to say something like Whatever did this it Was Not Of This World.' There was the tail end of a riotous, vari-coloured STAR TREK—THE MOVIE parade going by in the street but the definitely Oriental-looking Captain Kirk on the flying bridge of The Enterprise carrying truck failed to take his attention, 'But as a matter of fact, what did it was petrol.'

Constables Lee and Sun were inside the roped off police cordon watching the crowd in case they broke through. Captain Kirk, as the truck made its five miles an hour progress through the throng, yelled out, 'Warp factor ten, Mr Sulu!' and Sun and Lee, neither of them television watchers, looked confused. Macarthur said, 'According to the surviving sweeper, first he hit the saucer and then, for no apparent reason, the dead man.' The smell of burned wood and flesh was still in the air, 'He said there was a hissing or a clicking sound?'

'Yes.'

Macarthur nodded. 'The hissing was the propellant. The click was probably the ignition system setting off the flow from the muzzle.' He glanced over at the first street sweeper looking down at the charred broom. What little had remained of his colleague had been taken away in an ambulance and there was only the burnt bitumen by the broom to show where he had been. Macarthur said, 'Some sort of flame thrower or petrol gun. Judging by the total body incineration I'd say the spray was atomised into a fine mist before it was ignited.' He looked over with interest at a clutch of mini-skirted female members of the Star Trek crew on the back of the truck, 'Probably nothing more involved than a bigger version of a gas lighter. You could make a small metal tank with a tube attached to the gun, build in an on-off valve, put the petrol in the tank under high pressure and you'd have it.' He said a little sheepishly, 'I've been approached by quite a few film companies to be technical advisor on some of their new projects.' He forestalled Feiffer's question, 'As for the propellant, you could take an ordinary car tyre to a garage, pump it up to breaking point, and then bleed the pressurised air into the home-made tank.' Macarthur said with a shrug, 'On balance—'

On balance, it might have been easier if The Spaceman had not been of this world. At least it might have cut down the possible list of petrol and high pressure air suppliers. Feiffer said, 'And the saucer?'

'Made of old tea chests. Plywood painted in no doubt, highly inflammable cheap paint.' Macarthur said expertly, practising for his role as technician to the film world, 'Plywood as you probably know is glued together out of thin sheets of veneer with, to say the least, highly burnable hot glue.' He looked at what remained of the saucer, 'It's hard to tell now, but the inside spars were probably constructed out of lightweight magnesium—which would have gone up like something approximating a large incendiary bomb.' Macarthur's gaze rested briefly on the silent sweeper staring down at the broom, 'No personal motive involved, do you think?'

The street sweeper looked up from the broom and into Feiffer's face. The street sweeper asked, 'Mister, how could something like that happen?' He had tears glistening in his eyes, 'He was a friend of mine. He'd been on the job for almost twenty years.' He looked down at the broom, 'He worked hard! He may not have looked like he was working hard, but he always did the streets the Department told him to. Nobody ever complained.' He asked as a cheer went up from the crowd at the appearance of Mr Spock on The Enterprise's bridge, 'I thought things were supposed to work!'

Feiffer said, 'I'll have one of my Constables—'

'Things are supposed to work, Mister!' He looked over at the mocked-up computers and hardware on The Enterprise's cardboard bridge, 'You see things on television and they work!' He clutched Feiffer's arm as a thought occurred to him, 'We weren't loafing, Mister, we just walked across to see the flying saucer—we thought it might need a bit of sweeping done!'

Feiffer nodded.

'The Department—they'll think we were—'

'I'll fix it with the Cleansing Department—'

The street sweeper said, 'He was a working man, like me!' A deep 'Aiiya!' went up from the crowd as a procession of mutants and monsters following in the wake of the truck grunted and wrestled with each other over the charms of a six foot tall European model in glittering gold boots and an onyx studded leather suit. The sweeper shrieked out abruptly to the crowd, *'My friend was killed!'*

Feiffer caught Constable Sun's eye for an instant and motioned for him to come over.

The street sweeper said urgently, 'He wasn't real! He couldn't have been real! If he had been real he wouldn't have had a wooden saucer, he would have had a real one! That's why we went up to him—because we knew he wasn't real! We thought it was a machine. You see

15

machines on television and they work! They don't suddenly go mad and—' He plucked at Feiffer's arm with a strange, intense light in his eyes. He pointed at the truck carrying The Enterprise, 'That's a machine! Machines just don't go wrong. Do they? Mister?'

Feiffer glanced down at the charred broom, 'Sometimes.'

'Is that what happened? Did it go wrong?' The street sweeper said vaguely, 'My sister in law was going to save up and buy a washing machine, but her husband said they go wrong, but on television when you see them they always—' He asked, 'Do they go wrong, Mister? Machines? I've never owned one.'

'It was a man.'

The sweeper nodded. 'A spaceman. It was a machine dressed up to look like a—'

'It was a real man.'

The street sweeper shook his head, 'No.'

Feiffer touched at Sun's shoulder and brought him over next to the sweeper. Sun said gently to the sweeper, 'Come on, I'll take you home and you can give me a proper statement there. The car's in the next street.'

The sweeper said, 'No!' A look of horror came to his face, 'No, I'm not getting into a machine—no!!'

Feiffer clutched at the man's arm, 'It wasn't a machine. It was a man.'

'No!' The sweeper shouted above the noise of the crowd, 'No! A man wouldn't have done something like that! It was a machine!'

Sun said gently, 'Come on, I'll drive you home and—'

'NO!!' The street sweeper broke away and rushed into the crowd and was almost run down by The Enterprise truck reversing to go down an alley on its way towards Yellowthread Street and Galaxy Four, just a short drive away into the next, machine-abundant future.

*

On the phone O'Yee said desperately, 'Look, I had my mind on other things.' His wife was working herself up into one of her early morning tirades and he lit a cigarette nervously, 'Things like—'

'Like what? Like giving a home to every rapist, child molester and mugger in Hong Bay? Why don't you just put up a sort of doctor's sign reading *The Policeman Is Out?*' She paused only briefly to draw breath, 'It isn't enough, Christopher, that half the time I don't know when you're on duty or off or that the children have started asking me who that strange man shaving in the bathroom is, now you have to go off at 5 a.m. in the pitch dark and leave the front door open! *Do you know what sort of people there are in this district at 5 o'clock in the morning?*'

'Of course I know! I arrest them, remember?' She was going to say, 'Not fast enough.' O'Yee said, 'I checked around before I left.'

'If you checked around before you left why did you leave the door open? As a signal the coast was clear?' Emily O'Yee asked in that quiet, ominous, vaguely maternal Chinese voice of hers, 'Christopher, I realise that where you grew up in San Francisco, violent crime has never been heard of—'

'*I'm sorry, all right!*' O'Yee had a stroke of genius, 'I—I had my mind on other things, on your birthday, on—'

Emily O'Yee said in a voice so cold the receiver in his hand went white with icicles, 'It doesn't happen to be my birthday for almost three months.'

'I know. I know that. But I—but I've got something so good that I thought you could—' He felt the Detectives' Room filling up with water to nostrils level, 'I thought it was so good that I'd give you your gift early!' He drew a breath as the water receded in the silence and said, 'Phew!'

'Oh, yes?' The voice was sweet. Then the axe fell. 'Like ... *what?*'

Like. O'Yee said, 'Like ... ' O'Yee said in a burst, 'Like

free tickets to one of the big sci fi movie premieres tomorrow night. Like—I—I knew you liked sci fi movies and when I got offered some tickets for one of the premieres I knew you'd like to go and since the tickets included the kids I thought, wouldn't it be a good thing for all of us to—to make it your birthday present even though your birthday is really, actually—' He was babbling. He asked, 'Well, what do you think of that?' He said, running down like an alarm clock, 'I got them from a friend.'

Emily O'Yee said, awed, 'Really? You actually got tickets to—But everyone is going to be there: the Governor and film stars and—' She fell silent, 'And film stars and … and film stars and … '

O'Yee said, 'Right! Right! That's who I got them from—from a film star I just happen to know.'

'You never told me you knew a film star!' Emily O'Yee demanded, the neighbours already as good as informed, gloated at, and put in their rightful places forever, 'Who? Who do you know? Tell me who it is.'

O'Yee said, 'Um—' He thought fast, 'I can't. It's a secret. He's in one of the films in make-up and he doesn't want anyone to know who he is because he's been offered a serious part in a French film and he—' The whole thing was going with a frightening facility. O'Yee said before he turned into Baron Munchausen on the spot, 'I can't say any more.' Nothing was going to get him in any deeper, 'I swore to him I wouldn't tell a living soul who he is.'

Emily O'Yee said, 'Who is he?'

O'Yee said, 'The Green Slime.'

Emily O'Yee said in a tone of deep shame, 'And I rang you up to abuse you. All the time you've been thinking of nothing else but making your family happy and all I can do is ring you up and—'

O'Yee said magnanimously, 'I understand.' It was nothing. O'Yee said shrugging, 'Well, you know how it is. I'm in a position to do a few favours for people from time

18

to time and if I can help a fellow human being like a film star I don't see why I—'

Emily O'Yee said in a comradely voice, 'No wonder everyone likes you so much.' (O'Yee said, 'Oh, shucks ... ') 'Your friends must really—'

O'Yee said, 'Yeah.'

'I'm really sorry I bothered you, Christopher.'

O'Yee said, shrugging, 'Oh, no bother.'

Emily said happily, 'And he's really a friend of yours? You really have a friend like that? A real, live *film star?*' She said in a little girl's voice (so much for Women's Lib when it came to Chinese movie-mania), *'Gosh,* wait until I tell the children!'

From down in the cells, The Green Slime yelled out in a lather of attention-getting hysteria, 'YOU FILTHY GANG OF SLOP-EATING PIG COPS, YOU SHOULD ALL BE FLAYED ALIVE AND THEN THROWN TO THE DOGS!'

Friends? Sure, he had lots of them.

He wished to God he could think where a few of them were this morning.

*

The parade had moved on, and, with only passing glances at the tall fair-haired European watching a uniformed Constable take a street sweeper away for space-truck obstruction or something, the crowd had broken up and drifted away in search of other, more interesting spectacles.

A voice said softly in American-accented English, 'I was waiting until everyone had gone.' The voice asked, 'Chief Inspector Feiffer, isn't it?'

'Yes?'

The voice belonged to a well-dressed young man holding his hands nervously against the front of his light blue shirt and matching tie. 'Anthony Lam, currently the general manager of the Empress of India hotel, Hong Kong.' He paused and gave Feiffer a nervous smile, 'In whose employees' carpark we are presently standing.' He glanced down at the melted bitumen and then across to what was left of the flying saucer. There was another, similarly dressed Chinese standing a little behind him, 'My friend, Mr Teddy Wong of Hong Bay.' Anthony Lam said with his voice carefully low and secretive, 'Mr Feiffer, Mr Wong and I—we believe The Spaceman was not of this world.'

Another lunatic. Feiffer said softly under his breath, 'Shit ... '

Teddy Wong came forward. He also had a nervous smile on his face. His voice was firmer. He said quickly, 'What Mr Lam means is that we think The Spaceman came from *somewhere else.*'

Feiffer nodded. Somewhere among the information sheets at the Station was a cop's guide to the birthplaces of the forces that controlled the demented. Venus, he seemed to recall, was for schizophrenics, Mars for psychotics, obsessional neurotics favoured the dark side of the Moon for the controllers of their destiny, and Beyond The Stars, that one was the exclusive property – research had shown – of the ... Feiffer said wearily, 'Oh, yes. And where exactly do you think he came from?' He glanced across to see Macarthur walking towards his car touching at his body snatchers badge and no doubt thinking happily of the afternoon's clutch of post-mortems and dissections.

Anthony Lam said, 'Exactly?' He paused to put a specific location on it, 'I can't be really *exact*—'

Feiffer said, 'No.'

Anthony Lam said definitely, evenly, and very sanely, 'But, almost without doubt, certainly *somewhere* on the island of Singapore.'

He turned to Teddy Wong with a nervous smile on his face, relieved that at last he seemed to have captured the policeman's full and undivided attention.

3

In the three storey carpark in Canton Road, a brown Volkswagen kombi van halted at the ticket barrier while the driver, a young Chinese, reached over to the dispensing machine for a ticket while Detective Inspector Bill Spencer, a slightly frazzled European, leaned over to the brown kombi van and examined it to see what colour it was.

It was brown. He leaned back into the ticket office as the driver stared into his side view mirror to see if his petrol cap was still there, and said to Detective Inspector Auden and the ticket collector, 'It's brown.'

The ticket collector, a young fresh-faced German named Klaus, said softly in English, 'You don't say?' pressed a button on his console to open the barrier, and then, as the Volkswagen went through, pressed another to lower it again.

An exiting car on the other side of the office revved up its engine and Klaus leaned out to take the money and the ticket, inserted the ticket into a slot in his console and pressed up the barrier on the other side.

Detective Inspector Phil Auden was at a closed circuit television screen pressing buttons looking, unlike Spencer, not in the least frazzled. Each of the buttons activated a different camera: first the right hand side bays on the third floor, then, the left, the left hand bays on the second floor ... He pressed a button marked *Throughways,* sent the

21

screen into a frenzy of lines, then, pressing a button marked *2 to 3 centre*, brought up a picture of the brown Volkswagen driving up to the top floor in search of a vacant space and said with admiration, 'You could make a movie with one of these things.' He pressed the button marked *Ground Floor Central Throughway to Exit*, saw a blue Fiat 600 chugging its silent way towards him on screen, read its licence number, peered at the occupants, a Chinese woman and a child, and then, as the Fiat appeared in real life by the ticket barrier and paid up to leave, said, impressed, 'You could have one of these in your house.' He paused for a long fantasising moment, 'You know, in the spare bedroom or something.'

Spencer said disapprovingly, 'You don't have a spare bedroom.'

'Well, if I did!'

Klaus leaned past Auden and pressed the button marked *Ground Floor Right* and counted the empty spaces. A red Ford Escort paused at the ticket dispenser and, as the barrier raised, halted for a moment.

Klaus pressed a button and a ground floor plan of the carpark appeared on a display screen above the Ford showing a moving arrow pointing to the right.

The Ford went off into the ground floor cavern, circled around once, (Auden sat at the screen pressing buttons), and, as Auden urged the picture, 'There! Just there! No, reverse—a little further to the left ... fine ... fine ... ' found a safe haven.

A vehicle stopped at the barrier and Spencer leaned out of the ticket window to check if it was a yellow Volkswagen kombi van. It wasn't.

Auden said irritably, pressing a button, 'What are you leaning out for? You can see what it is from here by just pressing a button.' He asked Klaus, 'What do you think of this Gunfighter Game you see around? You know, the one where you try and shoot an electronic cowboy and if you get him it writes up on the screen "Got me!" Do you know that one?'

Klaus took the money from an exiting car and raised the barrier. He nodded. 'Yeah, they had those in Dublin.'

Spencer said, 'That's the trouble with people these days: they spend too much time sitting inside watching television screens when they should be out playing sport or doing something healthy.'

Auden asked, 'What were you doing in Dublin?'

'I used to live in Dublin. My father was an attaché at the German Embassy there.' Klaus gave Auden a resigned look, 'And before that in Belgium, and before that ... ' He shrugged, 'At the moment, I'm saving up to go to Australia. By ship. As soon as I've got enough money together I can sit down and invent something.'

Auden said, 'Yeah? Like what?'

'Something electronic. As soon as I find a country where there's something they need they don't have I'm going to invent it and—' His voice trailed off, 'You know, something electronic.'

A van was coming down the passageway from the street towards the ticket dispenser. Spencer ducked his head out before Auden could press his button and said quickly, 'It's a green Renault.'

Klaus said sadly, 'I offered to invent a computer set-up for the carpark here. You know, with magnetic strips on all the parking bays and a central decision console tied into a couple of automated display panels and barriers' – he pressed a series of buttons, located an empty space on the second floor and punched up the carpark plan with an arrow on floor two for the Renault – 'But the guys who own it say Kansas City here has gone about as far as it can go with TV screens and anyway people don't like automated carparks.' He shrugged again and pressed a button to turn off the direction board. 'The trouble about being an unqualified genius—nobody will give you a job worthy of your talents. So you have to invent something. And half the time—'

Auden glanced at the bank of buttons, 'Are you a genius?'

'Sure.' Klaus said earnestly, 'The trouble about being educated all over the world is that you never get the bits of paper that qualify you to work in any single one of them. If I'd grown up in one country I'd have been able to get all my papers and—' He shrugged, 'I'm like The Flying Dutchman, I just—' He asked Auden abruptly, 'Do you know anything about Australia? That's where I'm going next.'

Auden said, 'It's hot.'

A car came in from the street and Spencer The Sporting ducked out quickly to see what colour it was.

Auden said with distaste, 'And they're all health-mad. Pity you didn't invent The Gunfighter Game. That was really good.'

'My father was the ambassador to the Vatican when that came out. They don't go in much for gunfights in the Holy See.'

Spencer said, 'Cream Mosvich sedan.' There was a hum as Klaus put up the arrow board and the schematic outline to floor two.

Auden said, 'Fascinating.'

No yellow kombi van coming in. There had been six muggings in the last two days in the carpark, all on the second floor, all done by an unidentified mugger wielding a car window smashing iron bar. Six times the victims had appeared at the ticket booth covered in glass minus their cameras, purses, tape recorders and shopping parcels. Six times, the unidentified mugger had escaped in a yellow kombi van.

Six times Auden and Spencer had searched every inch of the carpark.

A vehicle came in and Spencer bobbed his head out quickly to scrutinise it.

24

No yellow kombi van coming in.

Hardly surprising since the thing, after each of the muggings, had never come out.

The disappearing one ton, fourteen foot long yellow Volkswagen kombi van.

Auden pressed a button, brought up a picture of the cream Mosvich sedan finding a spot on the second floor, wanted to hear more about the Gunfighter Game, and said to the bank of camera buttons and controls under his hand, 'Fascinating.'

A car halted at the exit barrier and before Spencer could get across to the window to peer out, Auden said off-handedly from his screen, 'Alfa-Romeo sedan, local Hong Kong licence plate; colour green; occupants, one male, one female and one kid.'

He said with genuine admiration for the strides Man no longer had to make in the twentieth century, 'Fascinating. Absolutely bloody fascinating.'

*

There was the faintest of faint tappings at the door of the Detectives' Room.

It was The Green Slime.

In all his rubber-tentacled, suckered and assorted rubber frog-featured glory, The Slime said happily in English, 'Hey, guess what?'

O'Yee said in a strangled voice, '—what?'

The Slime said, 'I've escaped.'

He gave O'Yee what approximated to a happy wink, and grinning expectantly, picked up his tail to swish over towards him for a chat.

*

The Spaceman had a small tissue-paper covered photograph concealed in the palm of his hand. Using his fingers dextrously, he turned it over unseen.

It was a head and shoulders picture of a European, evidently cut from a larger candid street shot with a line of Chinese characters on the back and, next to them on the left, a three digit number serving as a signature.

The characters, in translation, read: *Detective Chief Inspector Harry Feiffer, Yellowthread Street Station, Hong Bay,* and the numbers: *426.*

The number, that was the important part.

The Spaceman, dressed in civilian clothes, feeling safe, turned the photograph over again and, in the deserted service basement of the Empress of India hotel, snapped it hard like an Ace of Spades death card.

He smiled to himself as the square of cardboard made a sharp, echoing *click!* against his thumbnail.

4

In his office across the foyer from the front desk of the
Empress of India hotel Anthony Lam fingered a plastic
lapel card reading YOUR FRIENDLY MANAGER,
snapped it against his thumb, and putting it in his pocket
and gazing down at his hand to see if the thumbnail had
picked up any lint, said thoughtfully, 'I want you to
understand from the outset that I was educated in America
and I know what paranoia means. And I am definitely not
paranoid. Paranoia has to do with delusions of persecution
and I don't have those sort of delusions; I *am* being
persecuted.' He was choosing his words very carefully, but
they all seemed to be coming out the wrong way. He
lowered his voice, 'I also know what folie à deux means—'

Teddy Wong said with a smile, 'That's connected with
schizophrenia, Anthony—'

'—and Teddy Wong also knows I'm being persecuted
and Teddy is not crazy either.' Lam swallowed and looked
at Feiffer's face. It was bland. 'Teddy is the director of the
Foochow Insurance Company here in Hong Bay and he is
not therefore the sort of person to go off the rails even if I
am.' He looked down at his thumbnail again and scored it
deeply into the material of his trouser leg, 'And I'm not. I
know that something like five percent of all living human
beings are crazy, but I'm not one of them.' There were
tears brimming in his eyes, 'Teddy spends all his life with
statistics and he can tell you that, statistically, the chances

of my being one of that five percent, are – are percentage-wise, less than—'

Teddy Wong said gently, 'Take it easy, Tony ... '

'I am simply trying to convince Mr Feiffer here that I am not crazy!'

'Then you're trying too hard. Just tell him what you know and let him—'

Lam said, 'You get a lot of lunatics in your job, Mr Feiffer. Am I right?'

Feiffer looked at him dubiously. He nodded.

Well, I am not one of them!' Lam's mouth was quivering. 'Everything is goddamn backwards and any way I tell it makes me sound like some sort of madman who should be locked up in a rubber room. But I am not!' He was sitting opposite Feiffer at his desk. He put his clenched fist against his chin, 'Mr Feiffer, the reason I asked Mr Wong to be here with me is because, being in commercial insurance, he understands big business and he can make it clear that things that are happening are perfectly normal if you understand big business and if you understand big business then—'

Teddy Wong said quickly, 'The hotel, Mr Feiffer, is owned by a consortium of businessmen in Singapore.'

Anthony Lam said desperately, 'Maybe I *am* going fucking mad. Maybe I've just invented all this and I really am going—'

Feiffer said to Wong, 'And?'

'And the fact of the matter is that Mr Lam here was put in directly from hotel school to manage it for them. The Empress of India, as you probably know, before it was modernised, was famous as one of the great hotels of the world, like Raffles or Shepheard's in Cairo or—'

Feiffer nodded.

'And if you knew Hong Kong at all, you'll know that it has a history going back almost a hundred years—'

Feiffer nodded. 'I used to come here with my parents for Sunday lunch.'

Anthony Lam said suddenly, 'You did? Did you really?' He glanced at Teddy Wong with tears in his eyes, 'Oh my God, he might actually believe it!' He entreated Wong, 'For God's sake tell him—don't leave anything out!'

Wong nodded soothingly. 'There've been a number of acts of sabotage in the hotel recently – malfunctioning equipment, rats introduced into the kitchens, that sort of thing – general loss of revenue and good-will.'

Feiffer asked, 'And you insure the hotel against it?'

'No.'

Lam said suddenly, 'Insure this hotel? My God, he wouldn't!'

Wong shook his head. 'No, Tony, I told you: it isn't a question of wouldn't—I *couldn't.*' He turned to Feiffer, 'My firm is too small to take on a long term risk on that scale. We haven't the invested capital to cover it.'

Lam demanded, 'But if you could – tell him the truth – *would you?*'

'No.'

'You see, that proves it! We can't both be goddamned crazy, can we?'

If this one had been in the cop's guide to understanding lunatics it must have been in the sections he hadn't read. Feiffer said evenly to Wong, 'I'm still listening.'

'Well, the point is that the hotel is in a very good location. And for the last hundred years or so, regularly, it has made a very handsome profit for whoever owned it at the time. A prime investment.'

Lam said quietly, 'When it was the old style hotel. Before the old style hotel was torn down to make way for this glass and aluminium monstrosity!'

Wong ignored him. His tone was patient. 'And it still makes a profit.' He gave Anthony Lam an apologetic smile, 'Mr Lam was put in here straight from hotel school for one simple reason—'

Lam said softly, 'Yeah. It was because I was incompetent.' He looked at Wong for confirmation.

Wong said easily, 'Right.'

'I came last in my class at hotel school and everyone thought I was so completely and unemployably incompetent my teacher told me that if ever I got a job managing a goddamned take-away food stall in the goddamned street I'd still be employed two rungs beyond my capacity!' He snarled vehemently, 'And then those bastards in Singapore built this ten million dollar hotel and put me in sole, complete and total charge of it and sat back to laugh.' His voice was rising, 'But I fooled them because I was just as stupid as my clientele and they loved me!' He said in a fake mania that bordered perilously close to the real thing, 'Ha, ha, ha, HA!'

Teddy Wong smiled at him. 'Tony was a late developer.'

The cop's guide had definitely missed that one. Feiffer said, confused, 'Are you telling me that they put Mr Lam in to lose money?'

Wong said, 'Right first time.'

'Why?'

'So they could *make* money.'

Lam's voice came out of the dark recesses of madness, 'Wonderful, isn't it? Feel you're losing your mind, do you? Feel people are trying to persecute you, do you? Get the distinct impression that all this isn't going on anywhere except in your head, do you?' He was on the brink, 'THAT'S HOW I FEEL!'

Teddy Wong said, 'The hotel is a tax loss. Tony – for one reason or another – is making his backers a fortune.'

Lam said with a wild look in his eye, 'It was their idea to put up the Sci Fi convention in the hotel because they thought people like that were all madmen and they'd wreck the place and decent people would never stay here again, but I'm an ordinary decent person myself and I like science fiction movies and I—'

30

Teddy Wong, evidently the best friend Lam had ever had, said charitably, 'Tony has the common touch.'

'Right! I'm as common as dirt, but what I like everyone else likes because everyone else is as common as dirt too.' He demanded, 'Mr Feiffer, do you like science fiction and horror movies?'

'Yes.'

'So does everybody else! Q. E. goddamn D! Those fat cats in Singapore with their second class snobbery thought that no one of any quality would ever use a hotel where the management let in people dressed as monsters, but the fact of the matter is that everyone these days is so goddamn bored with intimidating head waiters and snobbery that they—' He left the sentence unfinished, 'I could never learn to read a French menu and so when ordinary, good, decent people come in we give them the French menu in—*in English!*' He put his elbow in his desk and stabbed his finger in the direction of the door to the main foyer, 'The whole world is full of stupid slobs and it's a relief for them to find out that when they drop the phoney accent and the manners everyone else in the world is just as slobbish as they are!'

Feiffer said blankly, 'Oh.'

Wong said, 'Well, in any event, it's a very good location for a hotel.'

'And what you're leading up to is that the so-called Singapore money men want to close the hotel down. Is that right?'

Lam said with a strange look in his eyes, 'Right. But they can't. It's listed as one of the best hotels in Asia. And it makes a fortune. If they closed it down they'd be just throwing away money.'

'But you said it was a tax loss. Surely if—'

Lam said, 'If they closed down the hotel they'd be losing a fortune.'

'But, again, if it's a tax loss enterprise then—'

31

Wong said, 'Ah, the fortune they'd lose wouldn't be in money, but in prestige. Prestige is money. If it was known they'd closed down a money-making proposition who'd invest with them on their other lucrative deals?'

Feiffer felt he was picking his way through a minefield labelled The Intricacies Of Asian Commerce. 'So what they want is for the hotel to cease trading for some other reason, is that right?'

Lam said, 'Right. Preferably because the new manager – me – was incompetent!'

'Which you aren't.'

'Ha! Which I'm not.' Lam said in happy amazement to Teddy Wong, 'He's listening! He's actually listening! It actually makes sense to someone in the real world! Someone is actually listening and understanding it!'

'So what you're leading up to is that The Spaceman is some sort of mad psycho employed by the Singapore men to—to do what? Burn the place to the ground. The owners would be the first people the police suspected.'

Wong said, nodding his head, 'Right.' He gave Feiffer a slow smile, 'Which is exactly why the police have to think he is just a mad psycho or that—'

Feiffer said, 'Or that what?'

'Or that he's after the million dollars.'

'What million dollars?'

Teddy Wong said, 'The million dollars out on display in the foyer.' He drew a breath, 'Outside in the foyer of this hotel, in the midst of the crowd you saw as you came in, there is one million American dollars in cash in a glass case. It is supposed to represent, for the interest of the guests and for publicity purposes, the cost of exactly ten minutes filming for one of the big sci fi movies being premiered tomorrow night. That is what The Spaceman is supposed to be after—the money.'

'Whose money is it?'

Lam said, 'Ah!!' Obviously, this was the clincher. Lam

said, *'It's the Singapore backers' money!'*

'But why would they want their own money stolen?'

Wong said, 'Because it's insured!'

Feiffer said, 'By whom?'

Wong said, 'By me! First The Spaceman makes his presence known, then he steals the money, then he burns the hotel down to the ground, then he—' He demanded, 'Can't you see that? *The million dollars is insured!* In the fire nobody would even know it had gone!' He asked, 'Why else? Why else would he use a flame thrower? Why else?'

Spacemen, flying saucers, Science Fiction and Horror movie congresses, Batman, Robin, The Green Slime, Lam, Wong, tax losses, million dollars ...

Lam said anxiously, 'Aren't you grateful? We've given you the solution to the whole thing straight off.' He seemed momentarily very happy.

Feiffer said weakly, 'Yes, thanks very much indeed.' He drew a breath, reached over for Lam's telephone on the desk, and thought the very least he could do in return, if the million dollars existed at all, was to get someone to guard it.

Anthony Lam had the same strange, mad light still in his eyes. He looked over at his friend Teddy Wong and grinned at him expectantly.

*

'How the hell can you have escaped when you were never even officially arrested in the first place?'

'If I was never arrested what was I doing in a cell?'

'I don't know what you were doing in a cell! That's because I don't know what you were arrested *for!*'

The Slime took a threatening swish forward, 'Don't you threaten me with violence—I'm giving myself up!'

'You can't give yourself up! You were never officially *taken in!*'

'I was in!'

'I know you were in! What I don't know is what you were in *for!*'

'Are you asking *me* what I was in for?'

'Yes!'

The Slime said, 'Nothing!'

'What do you mean, "Nothing"? You must have been in for something! I don't know if you're an axe murderer or a goddamned indecent exposure artist or a bank robber or a goddamned jaywalker!'

The Slime said, in disgust, 'Great! Typical cop. You just assume I'm some sort of criminal degenerate, don't you? It never occurs to you what I could really be, does it? You just assume I'm—'

'Forgive me! Tell me what you are!' O'Yee said desperately, 'Please!'

'What am I?'

'Yes!'

The Slime drew himself up to his full, hunched up green height. The Slime said with his horned chin held high, 'I, as a matter of fact, am—'

'Yes? Yes?'

The Slime yelled at the top of his voice, 'Innocent, that's what I am—*innocent!*' He lowered his voice as a cacophony of yells, mug bangings and chaos erupted from Batman and his friends downstairs in the lock-up, 'Don't trouble yourself to get up. I'll go back to my cell myself and await – very pessimistically – the unlikely appearance of some sort of *justice* in this town.'

There was an odd, anxious look for a moment in The Slime's eyes as if he was playing some sort of part difficult to maintain, but before O'Yee saw it, The Slime turned and, with a swish of his rubber tail, was gone again.

The keys to the cells were in O'Yee's desk drawer. He took them out and, getting up, glanced for a long moment at the telephone and sighed.

5

Field Guide To The Glazed Million Dollar Watcher (vertebrate, omnivore, genus Oriental)
Main Groupings:

(i) *The Dental Patient.* Notes: This most commonly noted member of the species is marked by its habit of letting its mouth fall open in the presence of one million American dollars and by its habit of clasping its hands loosely together at about nether region level [suggesting some psychosexual connection with the million dollars (see Rascovich: Random Notes On The Psychosexual Stance. The Million Dollar Watcher, *Nature*, 1 (iv) 1948).]
Call: a soft intake of breath and expulsion as: "Aii—ya ... !"

(ii) *The Weather Commentator.* Notes: a further grouping of the main species. Hands usually clasped in mantis-like attitude beneath beak region. Marked by its *Call,* which approximates that of a fat man blowing on a hot day. ("Whew-wee ... !") Literature: Transcript BBC radio programme, July 19, 1931: The Weather Commentator, The First Sightings Of Spring. (Out of print).

(iii) *The Cud Chewer:* the rarest of the million dollar watchers of the primary grouping, this creature when placed in the proximity of one million dollars becomes immediately mesmerised, its eyes remaining stationary in their orbits, the mouth making masticating movements. *Call:* (Oriental variety) "Heea, heea ... mm, mmm.mm ... " (North American and European variety:

noted by Held in field trip, 1975/6/7/8) "Christ, wow, hell ... !" and – more rarely – "Oh boy, sonofabitch, look at that ... "
Unconfirmed, study proceeding.

Anthony Lam said, 'One million dollars all in one hundred dollar notes.' The glass case was a cube about four foot square standing on a metal tripod, 'One hundred wads of one hundred dollar bills, each wad containing ten thousand dollars each.' He saw Feiffer's face, 'The case has a combination lock on it that you couldn't open with dynamite.' He was speaking in English, but it was evidently a language one or two of the Glazed Million Dollar Watchers could understand. They turned around to him with pained looks. 'It's the cost of approximately ten minutes filming time of one of the big science fiction movies they're premiering tomorrow.'

Wong had a wry grin on his face. He asked Feiffer in a hushed voice, 'Have you ever seen that much money in one place?'

A million dollars had a strange effect on people. Feiffer found himself smiling wistfully. 'I've never seen that much money in half a dozen places.' It was a field of green. In spite of himself, he moved forward a little towards the knot of worshippers and made a Cud Chewer noise with his mouth. (A Weather Commentator, a balding Chinese business-man in a fawn suit, drew a breath and said, 'Whew-wee!') 'What sort of security do you have on it?'

Lam said abruptly, 'We thought we had the *police*.' He indicated two or three of the larger sized coveters of plunder on the left of the case, 'I thought they were plain-clothes men.' (The plain-clothes men had looks on their faces that resembled the required looks of plain-clothes men about as much as Willy Sutton resembled J. Edgar Hoover.) Lam said, 'If the Singapore money men were honest they would have told you days ago.'

'I might say the same about you.' Feiffer glanced at Wong.

Wong said, 'I thought Tony had told you. I only realised this morning he hadn't.'

Lam had a twitch going under his eye, 'They're out to get me, I know they are!'

Wong said softly, 'Take it easy, Tony.' He gave Feiffer a quick encouraging grin, 'Mr Feiffer realises you're under a strain, but everything's all right now.' He said in a nanny-like voice to lullaby Lam off into peaceful thoughts, 'Mr Feiffer is getting some of his policemen here to guard it, aren't you, Mr Feiffer?'

Feiffer nodded. He saw Constables Lee and Sun come in by the front entrance and, once they got over their stunned first sight of the money, run through a quick mental list of schemes, projects, investment houses, banks and gold bullion they could put it into if it were theirs, contemplate turning to a life of crime and totting up the odds of getting away with it, and then settle themselves – judging by their faces, happily enough – on either side of the money.

Lam said in an undertone, 'It's the messages.'

Teddy Wong said, 'Sure.' He touched Lam on the arm, 'I wouldn't worry about that ... '

Feiffer said, 'What messages?'

Lam said again, 'The messages. I keep getting messages.' He had that same strange look in his eyes. He gazed at the money and blinked as if it was giving off strong rays, 'I keep getting messages. I wasn't going to tell you because Teddy said you might think I was—'

Feiffer exchanged a look with Wong. Wong shook his head and made an apologetic shrug. He patted Lam on the arm.

Lam's eyes were moving back and forth in their sockets, lost and vague. Retreating into his own little world, he said in an eerie child's tone of voice, 'Teddy said I shouldn't tell anyone, but it's true: I keep getting messages.' He went on before Feiffer could speak, 'And every time I get a message, it just ... it just disappears and no one believes me except me because I've seen it—' He shook his head sadly, 'Because it just disappears.' He sought Feiffer's eyes intensely, 'They trick me.'

Teddy Wong said quickly, 'Anthony's been under a strain with this Singapore business and then, with The Spaceman setting fire to the carpark this morning—'

Feiffer said directly to Lam, 'What messages? What do they say?'

Lam said softly, 'They're all written on water, the messages. On the windows in my office. It rains and words appear on the window and then ... it just washes off, and on mirrors and on cigarettes ... ' He seemed to be drifting away, 'On the cigarettes in my desk box. I light a cigarette and words appear on the paper with the heat and I ... I try to stub it out before it goes, but it just ... all burns away ... ' He opened and closed his mouth several times without forming words. 'And this morning, in my office bathroom, I—on the toilet basin, words, but then the—' He said with a sudden ferocity, 'I had to piss and when I did the words appeared on the toilet bowl and then' – he grasped Feiffer hard by the sleeve – 'But everyone knows, it's just force of habit, you just – automatically – you just flush it without thinking and the words—the words are all gone!' He said with savage intensity, 'I'm not mad! I'm not!'

The Dental Patients, Weather Commentators and Cud Chewers, acting coincidentally in single flock, said to the million dollars, 'Ohhh ... ' and shuffled around the case to change vantage points.

Teddy Wong seemed, for the second time that morning, embarrassed. He looked at Lam with an expression of concern on his face.

Feiffer said, 'But what messages? What did the messages say?'

Wong said soothingly, 'Come on, Tony, you probably imagined it all anyway. The main thing is that the police are here now and—'

38

The nervous tic was going non-stop under Lam's eye. He said softly, 'They said, all of them, *The Spaceman Is You.*' Lam said with a sad smile on his face, 'Maybe I should go mad. It might be better. Then I wouldn't think any of this was strange. Maybe I should just go mad—'

Teddy Wong said in friendship, 'Tony, Tony … '

Lam said softly, 'And then maybe I'd be happy.'

Feiffer asked cautiously, 'What language were the messages in? English or Chinese?'

Teddy Wong said quickly to lessen the effect, 'The Singapore backers are Chinese, Mr Feiffer, but that doesn't mean they couldn't have—'

Lam said softly, 'No, they weren't in English or Chinese.' He drew a breath, 'I was born in Singapore so I know. The messages were all in Malay.' He said with his eyes glazed and staring, 'I—I've been getting them now—for weeks—'

At the case, in their new positions, the watchers made a satisfied grunting sound.

*

In the Detectives' Room O'Yee looked down his hand written list of names and telephone numbers. The list began:

Porno Lillie Rodriguez
One Eared Hot Time Alice Ping
Dirty Elmo Fan
Flick Knife Fong The Fence
Hanford Hill Hing
Chester Chan
Bulldozer Boon
Ack-Ack Au Chark
Chainsaw Chu Teh …
… and more …

They were, without exception or mitigation, the most vicious, depraved, and totally degenerate, evil, anti-social, criminal element in the whole of Hong Bay and South East Asia and if anyone might have a few spare tickets to the big film premieres tomorrow night they would.

O'Yee was a policeman, a peace officer sworn to uphold the law, a guardian of the untrammeled and untroubled undisturbed progress of civilised order, and by God, when it came to dealing with scum like that, he knew exactly how to get from them just exactly what he wanted.

Lifting the telephone, he set his mouth into a firm line and prepared to fall on his knees and beg.

6

In the ticket office, Auden said in a harsh whisper, 'It's him!' He froze at the television screen as a yellow Volkswagen kombi van, next in line behind a Chrysler sedan, waited to be dispensed its ticket. He saw Spencer about to lean out of the window to make sure, 'Don't lean out! It's him! I can see it on the screen.' There was a pinging sound as the driver of the sedan took his ticket from the dispensing machine and, with a rev of its engine, the Volkswagen moved up.

Spencer stepped back into the ticket office out of sight. He saw the front of the Volkswagen. It was yellow. There were exhaust fumes swirling around as the driver tapped at the accelerator in neutral to keep the engine going.

The driver took his ticket. There was a pinging sound, then the barrier rose and the engine, revving high, chugged the long vehicle past the office (Spencer tried to see the driver's face, but he was looking up at the vacant spot indicator and was turned away), and then, with a roar, the vehicle headed towards the centre throughway to floor ...

Auden said quickly to Klaus, 'Where? Which floor did you direct him to?'

'Floor two, right!'

Auden punched up the throughway to floor two on the screen. The Volkswagen chugged onto the throughway in silent picture, swirled exhaust fumes as the driver changed

41

into a lower gear for the uphill climb, then began up the throughway.

Spencer had a long white coat in his hand. The coat had the legend *Canton Road Carpark* stencilled on it in English and Chinese. He put the coat on quickly and unclipped the safety thong on his belt holster to see if his gun moved freely in the leather. It did. The Volkswagen reached the top of the throughway, the driver paused for a moment, then went, not right, but left.

Auden said in a whisper, 'He's gone left!' He flicked at the buttons on the console and brought up a picture of the left hand bays. They were all full. The Volkswagen slowed down and began crawling at a snail's pace, the driver leaning slightly out of his window looking for something.

Auden said, 'He's looking for someone in their car.' He pressed a row of buttons and brought up in series floors one, two and three, then the right hand bay of level two. In the neon-lit bays of cars parked in rows like white bottles, he could see no one.

He pressed up the emergency fire exit on the screen.

No one. The door was still closed and sealed.

There was only one pedestrian entrance from the street and one exit, both by the ticket office. Auden tried to remember where the last car in had gone: a cream Mosvich. Auden asked Klaus, 'Quick, which floor did you send it to?'

'I don't remember.' Klaus asked, 'Is that the mugger? What's he doing?'

Spencer buttoned up his coat and started for the door.

Auden said, 'He's looking for someone getting into their car.' He said to Spencer, 'Wait until I see where he ends up.'

'He's on the second floor. There's only one way he can go without coming back and that's up.' Spencer said, 'I'm going.'

Auden said, 'He's stopped!'

'Get your coat on, Phil!'

'No, wait. We're better off here. We can see where he's going.' Auden pressed a button to see if he could get a reverse shot of the left hand side of the second floor by using the right hand cameras. He couldn't. He pressed back to the left hand cameras again. 'He's started off again. He's leaning out of the car looking for something.' There was a legend written on the side of the van, but he couldn't read it in the brightness of the lights in the bays. Auden said, 'He's reversing—he's stopped. He's going towards—' He pressed another button and brought up nothing but a row of cars. 'I've lost him again!' Klaus was standing above him, watching. Auden ordered him, 'Here, you're the expert: you do it!'

A car waiting by the exit barrier honked its horn in annoyance and hesitating, Klaus said, 'I have to take the money—'

Auden said, 'Screw the money!' He took Klaus by the sleeve and pulled his hand down to the buttons, 'Find him!'

Spencer said, 'Phil, this is ridiculous! We can get up there and catch him in the act—'

'I've got him in the act!'

Klaus pressed a button and the Volkswagen appeared on floor two, making for the central throughway up to the next level. Klaus pressed in the Central Throughway 2 – 3 button and caught a picture of the vehicle pausing in a haze of blue exhaust smoke.

Spencer had the door to the ticket office open.

Auden said, 'He's still on floor two. He's reversing back to—I can see that cream Mosvich. There's someone it it. A man. He's winding the window up before he gets out.' He pressed a button and got a better picture, 'Here comes the Volkswagen. It's seen him.' He said suddenly hushed, 'It's stopped!'

'Phil, this isn't television! This is real!' Spencer threw a second dust coat to Auden and, as Auden got up with a last glance at the screen, ran towards the throughway to the second floor.

Auden called back to Klaus as the honking from the waiting car reached a crescendo, 'What's happening? What's happening!'

Klaus, looking alarmed, yelled back, 'He's stopped the VW in the middle of the passageway and he's getting out with something in his hand!' The honking stopped for a moment as the driver of the waiting car, a middle-aged Chinese, wondered what an alarmed-looking car park attendant might be yelling out to two other dust jacketed attendants, drawing guns.

Drawing guns? The driver revved up his engine, to hell with the money and, if Klaus hadn't instantly stabbed the button to open the barrier, would have smashed it to matchwood in his panic to get out.

*

At the money, Constable Sun asked Feiffer as Anthony Lam and Teddy Wong went back in the direction of the manager's office, 'What do you think, sir, is he crazy?' There was a wild Vampire-like shriek from inside one of the bars across the foyer and then, following the Vampire shriek, a Vampire face and body swirled itself out of the entrance, found everyone too busy looking at money to think of garlic and gold crosses, and went back into the bar again and resumed shrieking in there.

Constable Lee had joined the knot of million dollar watchers. He touched at the heavy combination lock on the armour glass cube and the watchers around him went ecstatically, 'Ohh ... '

'I don't know. He claims he gets messages written on water and smoke. What do you think?' Feiffer watched the man's retreating back, 'I think I'd be slightly more certain of his stability if I'd heard about the messages *before* The Spaceman had appeared rather than after.' Lee rapped on the glass hard—it sounded like three inch thick tungsten steel. 'You and Lee stay here and keep an eye on the money.'

'Where will you be?'

'Companies Squad.' Feiffer said with sudden anxiety, 'Unless Doctor Macarthur is scheduling the sweeper's autopsy for today. Is he?'

'No, sir, I rang him after I took the other sweeper home. His office said he'd gone off to give technical advice to a movie company.' Sun volunteered, 'The surviving sweeper didn't tell me anymore than he told you: it was a man dressed in a silver spacesuit. I stopped on the way over to show him a few movie posters – they're showing *2001* over at the Roxy in Queen's Street – but he said it didn't look like the ones in the Kubrick film – he said it had a soft helmet.'

'More like ... what? A gas suit?'

Sun shrugged. 'He didn't know. I guess in his line of work he doesn't see too many spacesuits one way or the other. I got a neighbour to take him in. I've got his address if we need him.' Sun, gazing at the money, asked slowly, 'There's no possibility it could just be some sort of publicity stunt that went wrong, is there?'

'The sweeper told me that The Spaceman took aim. He told me he seemed to be waiting for someone.'

'At that time of the morning? To do what? Help him blow up a flying saucer? For what?'

Feiffer shook his head and looked over at the money. The hotel foyer and, he assumed, all the other floors, were carpeted in what looked like very thick, highly inflammable nylon carpet. He looked over towards the window: double drapes of the same material. And the ceilings: plasterwork, paint, and no doubt, under that plasterwork and paint, joists and battens of dry, soft, easily ignited wood. The hotel was a single column skyscraper shaped exactly, when you saw it from a distance, like a forced-draught chimney.

Sun said encouragingly, 'Maybe it was just something that went wrong. Maybe it was just meant to be the flying saucer, and the sweeper just—' He looked anxiously at the few fire extinguishers at intervals along the walls and then up at the sprinkler system, and said louder than he had intended, 'Sir, this place is right in the middle of the waterfront area. If it ever caught fire—'

Some of the watchers around the money had cigarettes in their hands. Feiffer watched as their smoke rose up, swirled around the ceiling, and then, dissipating, lay invisibly in the air currents.

Sun said self-soothingly, 'Maybe it was just a stunt and his Mummy has taken his little ray gun away from him and told him to spend the rest of the day inside.'

Maybe she had. The question was, in the mind of someone who had calmly turned that ray gun on someone and held the trigger down until he was dead, exactly where "inside" might be.

Feiffer looked at his watch. Noon.

Friday when the Congress broke up seemed like a very long way off.

*

Behind a pylon at the top of the throughway on the second floor, Spencer peered into the parking bays and said in a whisper, 'I can see him. He's standing by the van. He's got the van parked in the middle of the passageway blocking it. The engine's still running.' He saw the driver glance in his direction and then look away. 'He's got the iron bar in his hand wrapped up in white paper and he's looking in the direction of the Mosvich.' He tried to make out the Mosvich's driver, but there must have been a bulb out in the bay and from that angle, the man was only a shadow.

Auden, raising his Colt Python and snapping it open and then closed again to check the load, said urgently, 'We'll take him now.'

'No. I want to know how he does it. He's never actually hurt anybody. I want to know how he gets away without being seen.' He turned around and shook his head, 'I just don't understand how he got that van out yesterday without our seeing it.'

'Because we were wandering about searching for it in the bays when we should have been using the cameras!' Auden said in the most unlikely hypothesis of the century, 'He must have kept going up higher and higher in the levels as we searched them and then, when he got to the top floor—'

'Yes?'

Auden looked down at the gun. 'And then ... ' Auden said irritably, 'How the hell should I know? I'm a cop, not a bloody inventor of magic tricks!' He pushed past Spencer and peered out around the pylon and saw what he was looking for. 'The red light's on on the TV camera up there. The camera's watching him.'

'That doesn't do us any good.' Spencer saw the Volkswagen driver tap the bar harder against his hand impatiently, and then, deciding, go towards the Mosvich. Spencer said, 'He's going to do it ... ' He drew in a breath and edged around the pylon to nail the mugger in the act.

In the gloomy bay, the driver of the Mosvich, a jewellery salesman catching a few spare moments to smoke an untroubled cigarette, wound down his window and said to the Volkswagen driver in Cantonese, 'What? Oh—Sure.' He leaned forward to start his car.

The Volkswagen driver said, 'Thanks very much,' glanced over at his van to see if he had left the Mosvich driver enough room, and asked, 'Do you want me to direct you out?'

The Mosvich driver said, 'No,' and jerked his head with some pride at the little sticker on his windscreen informing the world that the vehicle bearing down on them was in the hands of not an ordinary, but an advanced driver. The Mosvich driver said, 'Everyone in this town ought to take one of those courses.' He started the engine, put the car into reverse, and as a stentorian voice coming from behind the biggest gun he had ever seen reflected in a rear view mirror or anywhere else, thundered, 'STAND STILL OR YOU'RE A DEAD MAN!' let out the clutch, pressed the accelerator in pure terror, and smashed out both his rear and braking lights against a pylon.

The gun was directed at the Volkswagen driver standing near the burnt out bay light. The Volkswagen driver dropped his replacement neon tube with a crash.

There was a little sign on the side of the idling Volkswagen. It said, first in Chinese and then in English, *Mong's Lighting Shop,* and then below it a list of some of the firms and organisations the said illustrious firm of Mong contracted to.

One of them read *Canton Street Multi Storey Carpark.*

Auden lowered the gun.

Spencer said, 'Gosh, we're awfully—' There was a man coming towards him from the throughway to the third floor and he holstered his revolver and went forward to pacify him. Spencer said quickly, 'It's all right. We're police. There's nothing to—'

The man was covered in smashed window glass. Halting for a moment to take in the scene, he shouted at the top of his lungs in Cantonese, 'If you're the cops what the hell are you doing down here with a yellow Volkswagen?' There was a faint trickle of blood on one of his cheeks.

The man yelled out in the echoing, dank caverns of the second floor level, 'I've just been mugged on the third floor!' He stared at Auden with wide, disbelieving eyes. 'What the hell are you doing playing around here with a yellow Volkswagen? The one the mugger got away in was *blue!* Didn't you see? *It must have come right by you!'* He saw the smashed neon light tube on the ground and the look of shock on the face of that apprehended desperate character the neon light man. The bleeding man, driven to a fury, foamed, 'Is that what I pay taxes for? So you stupid cops can go around arresting fluorescent tube vandals?' The Mosvich driver got out of the Mosvich looking like an advanced driver who had just driven backwards into a stone pylon in a carpark.

The bleeding man demanded, hopping about like a sparrow, 'Well? *Well?'*

Evidently, as well as being able to do the greatest disappearing trick of all time, the mugger's yellow Volkswagen kombi van had another little wrinkle in its repertoire.

Evidently, when the need arose, or maybe when it just plain felt like it, it could also change colour.

In a shrill voice, the man from Mong's began to ask who was going to pay for the broken neon light tube.

*

On the phone, Porno Lillie Rodriguez said in cheery Cantonese, 'Miss Rodriguez Leather Goods And Whip-Testing Factory.'

There was a silence.

'No?' Lillie tried again, 'Miss Rodriguez's High-Heeled Shoe Emporium.'

Nothing.

'Rubberwear and Disciplining Corsets a speciality.'

The voice at the other end of the line cleared its throat and said, not 'Aii-ya', but rather: 'Um ... '

Porno Lillie changed to English, 'Southside Massage Parlour.'

The voice, definitely Chinese-American, said, 'Shit ... '

Lillie said, 'Victorian enemas without prescription.' The

49

voice was wavering. Lillie said quickly, 'We are all friends here.' Was it a West Coast accent? 'Happy friends and gay. Actually, to tell the truth, this is only an old theatrical costumiers a few friends of mine have taken over – and would you believe it? – the whole place is full of nothing but *racks and racks of Nazi uniforms and jackboots!* Much more of this and she was going to charge extra, 'Bondage? Flagellation? Paedophilia? Horses?'

O'Yee said softly, 'Movie tickets.'

Lillie said, 'Ah! To view, buy, rent, direct, or star in?'

Silence again.

O'Yee said, 'Science fiction.'

'To—'

O'Yee, chancing all, said directly, 'Look, Lillie, this is Christopher O'Yee down at Yellowthread Street – Senior Detective Inspector O'Yee – you remember: the understanding cop you told the sad story to about how if it hadn't been for this American sailor named Lieutenant Pinkerton you met in Japan once you wouldn't be in this sort of business – the understanding cop who let you off with a warning. What I want are a few tickets to the sci fi movie premieres tomorrow night. Any of the premieres will do. I'm prepared to pay for them and I'm prepared to be grateful to the person who sells them, but the fact of the matter is that my family thinks I've got tickets and if I don't get tickets—' There was a silence at the other end of the line and O'Yee said desperately, 'Lillie, are you still there? I swear to you this isn't some sort of entrapment, but if anyone can get hold of some tickets you can.' More silence. 'I'm not recording this conversation—what have you said anyway? Lillie, I'm begging you! I need those tickets!'

Lillie sighed. Everything these days with the cops was a freebie.

O'Yee said, 'Please, please—'

Lillie, sighing, said, '*NO!*'

'Please, Lillie, I know you can get them!'

'NO! NEVER! NEVER! NO! *NO—OO!*'

'You owe me!'

'O'Yee, I owe you nothing! I'm a cruel woman! I wouldn't spit on you if you were on fire! If you were dying of cancer I'd shove another cigarette in your mouth and light it! If you were dying of thirst I wouldn't give you a drop of my sweat! I'm a cruel, vicious, hard, nasty woman—hard, vicious and callous!' She said, '*Grrr!*'

'I'll pay!'

Damn right he would. Masochists. They were a good line in her business. Still, she did owe him maybe an extra little one.

Lillie said with enthusiasm, 'You dirty, low-life whining weasel, I wouldn't take money from you if it was coated in gold-dust!'

If you weren't careful, if you were a certain sort of person, you could learn to enjoy this sort of thing.

Lillie, ever the professional, hung up quickly before he did.

*

To the sounds of Batman throwing up in the next cell, The Green Slime sat on his bunk with his tail under him and put his chin on his chest to think. He had two small pieces of metal in his hands and he jangled them together and made a rhythmic clicking noise.

Getting up, he sighed and went towards the steel door to the cell, tapped the two pieces of metal against it, and, putting his arm out through the open grille plate set in at shoulder level, found the key-lever tumbler lock securing the door and inserted the smaller of the two pieces of metal into the keyhole and gave it a little twist.

The smaller of the two pieces of metal was a tension tool, a one eighth inch diameter rod about one and a half inches

51

long, pointed at one end. The Slime had an X-ray picture of the lock's interior in his mind. He moved the tension tool a fraction and saw rather than felt the point locate the key notch in the underside of the lock's main bolt.

Affixed to the bolt, the design of this particular lock featured a racking stump. The racking stump in this particular design controlled the action of the tumblers. The Slime, still holding the tension tool in place with his thumb and index finger, twisted his hand and brought the other tool – the pick – into play, inserted it into the keyway, found the tumbler taking the strain of the racking stump and moved the pick upwards.

There was a click as the first tumbler rose upwards towards the level of the racking stump and the first tumbler unlocked.

The Slime put a little pressure on the tension tool and located the next tumbler with his pick and raised that too. There were three gates in the tumblers that the racking stump had to align with and pass through in order to work.

The Slime, not even concentrating fully, found the third tumbler with his pick and gave it the slightest of upward pushes. He put his shoulder gently against the cell door and twisted his hand.

There was a sharp *click!*

Withdrawing his tools from the open lock, The Slime automatically wiped them on his hand to clean them, then, glancing down at them, threw them out of sight into the toilet bowl in the corner of the cell.

The two tools were nothing more than rusty nails he had found securing the legs of his bunk.

Their loss mattered not at all.

He could have picked the lock as easily using nothing but a piece of broken matchstick and an inch or two of doubled-over knotted string.

He went back to his bunk, and, with a look of rising anxiety on his face, tried to work out the best thing to do.

*

In the basement of the hotel, his eyes moving over the maze of pipes and fuse boxes on the walls, The Spaceman pulled on his silver suit and clipped it tight around his body with rivet studs. The boots came next. He pulled them on over his shoes and took a few exploratory, silent steps, then drew on his thick silver gloves and set the nozzle of the flame-gun firmly into the clips that held it in the palm of his right hand. The pressurised tank strapped to his forearm under the suit felt cold and frosty against his shirt. He touched it with his free hand and checked it was secure against leaks and movement.

He pressed the trigger of the gun gently and a hiss of high pressure air and petrol vapour rushed out in a pencil thin stream and dissipated.

The soft silver helmet with its black Perspex face plate was on the cement floor in front of him.

He leant down and took the helmet up and slipped it on over his head.

His breath under the face plate came in quick shallow gasps and, briefly, condensed on the inside of the Perspex.

Like an armoured knight about to go into battle, The Spaceman was prepared.

Shivering slightly with anticipation, he went forward, confident in his ability to succeed.

7

Seated luxuriously in a rattan armchair in the first floor Palm Court Bar of the Empress of India hotel, Henry Wu said, 'Worms.'

His partner, a well dressed Chinese named Charlie Kong, glancing at the elderly lady in twin set and pearls at an equally elderly grand piano in the otherwise deserted old style room, said, 'Been done.'

Wu said, 'O. K. ... ' The elderly lady began a loving rendition of *Fascination*, 'Tarantulas!'

'No.'

'Flies? Cobras? Apes? Vultures? *Trolls?*'

Kong said with a sigh, '*The Curse Of The Fly, The Return Of The Fly, The Giant Fly, Cobra Woman, Daughter Of Cobra Woman, Son of Cobra Woman, The Giant Ape, The Planet Of The Apes, Return To The Planet Of The Apes, The Vulture, The Planet Of The Vulture, The Prey Of The Vulture, I Was A Vulture—*'

Wu paused to think, '*The Day—*'

'*—The Earth Stood Still? Caught Fire? Met Its End? Broke Loose—*'

Wu had a cigar in his hand. He crushed it out in an ashtray on the table in front of him and looked irritated at the piano playing. '*Brains*—a fungus or monster is attacking brains and—'

Kong said with the faintest of faint smiles, 'You mean *Donovan's Brain?* Or *The Brain Eaters?* Or—'

'Not brains, *minds!*'

'*The Mind Benders? The Mind Of Mr Soames? Someone Has Control Of My Mind—?*'

Wu said with a snarl, 'What about a goddamned *silent* movie then? Surely to Christ that's original!'

Wong said, 'Like *I Was A Teenage Caveman? Homunculus? Five Million Years—*'

'A goddamned *nude* sci fi movie then!'

Kong said, '*Flesh For Frankenstein, The Southern California Naturist Horror, The Gene Stealer, Brides For The Aliens, Naked Moonmen—*'

'Set in Alaska?'

'*The Thing, Ice Age, The Nome Nightmare* ... '

Wu said, 'For the love of God, Charlie, there must be *something* new under the sun!'

Kong said without thinking, listening to the music, '*Solaris, The Ships Of The Sun, Sun Warriors, Sun Spot, Sun—*' He halted and gave Wu a happy smile, 'No, it looks like we're going to have to go along to the premieres again this year, see what's new and then before the audience interest dies off, do a quick rip-off movie along the same lines. The same as we always do every year.'

Wu gritted his teeth. For a moment, tears welled in his eyes.

Kong said, 'Look at it this way. We make a fortune on what's certain. Why take a chance with a new idea of our own?'

'Because I'm an artist and I've got my pride!' Lighting a Havana Corona with his gold Dunhill lighter and shooting the cuff of his Italian silk shirt Wu said with the intensity of a man used to starving in a garret for what he believed in, 'Giant snails! Comets! Leeches! Puppets, baboons, whales —*trees!*'

Kong said without effort, '*The Snails, The Giant Snails, The Leeches, Return Of The Leeches, Comet, Meteor, The Elmwood Virus, Oakfear, Walnut—*'

Wu said with feeling, 'Aw—Shit!'

Kong said, *'The Sewer Terror, Bacteria Creatures Beneath The Streets* ... '

He saw the elderly European woman at the piano smile at him and he nodded and raised his glass to her playing and felt good.

*

In the carpark ticket office, Spencer, his eyes purposely averted from the glowing television screen under Auden's control said, 'Furniture vans.'

Auden flicked a button and brought up the throughway from the second to the first floor on the screen. Auden said with a shake of his head, 'Impossible.' He touched another button and displayed the entrance to the carpark itself and the sign above the ticket office that warned prospective furniture van entrants *Headroom 6' 2" Only.* 'They'd have to come in with flat tyres to get under the ceiling.' He flicked another button and brought up another throughway.

'Then they're hiding behind another vehicle!'

Auden went flick, flick, flick. The cars on all the floors were parked in non-concealing one car sized bays. If the Kombi could hide behind there it would have had to have been, as well as colour-changeable and invisible, about two inches wide. Auden said, 'No.'

'Then it's getting up to the roof!'

Auden ran his hand over the rows of buttons on the camera-selection console. There was no camera for the roof. Auden said, 'A car can't get up to the roof. That's why there's no camera for it.' He went flick, flick, flick again and scanned the three floors in order, then brought up more throughways. Auden said, 'We missed him last time because we were following the neon tube man on camera. If we'd kept on scanning like this—'

Spencer said doggedly, 'One of us should be on patrol.' He saw a picture of the ticket office itself come up on the screen and looked away in disgust, 'That television wouldn't prove how the mugger's vehicle changes colour.'

Auden said casually, 'Simple. The last victim was colour blind.'

'The last victim wasn't colour blind! I asked him the colour of every car in the bay when I took his statement. He's no more colour blind than I am!'

Auden said, 'Hmm,' and flicked up another picture. He ran his hand exploratorily over a row of unmarked buttons and asked Klaus with interest, 'What are these ones for?'

Klaus leaned over. 'It's a standard console for a big building. Those buttons aren't connected to anything because this building is too small.' A car went out and he collected the money and opened the barrier, 'If you want my opinion, the owners would be a lot better off with a doppler system rather than television.'

Auden looked interested, 'What's that? A doppler?'

Spencer said, 'I don't happen to be colour blind either. I was tested at school.'

Auden said, dubiously, 'Properly? By a proper machine or just by—' Klaus was standing above him gazing at a picture of the first floor throughway and Auden asked him, 'You don't have one to show me, do you? One of those doppler things?'

Spencer said, piqued, 'The answer to everything isn't machines! I think we should get out of here and go on patrol in the carpark. I think we should try a little old fashioned *police work!*' He asked Klaus roughly, 'How do you know a car can't get up to the roof?'

Klaus said to Auden, 'It's a system whereby a sensor shoots out a sort of radar signal and then, a microsecond later, another and then another in a continuous series of two signal cycles. By comparing the echo from the different signals it can tell if anything's moved in the area it's targeting.' He said looking down at the screen and putting a gleam into Auden's eye, 'It's a much more impressive display than a television screen and if you tie it in to a simple computer it even makes the decisions about where to direct the cars for you.'

Auden said, 'Wow!'

Spencer said insistently, 'How do you know a car can't get up onto the roof?'

Klaus said evenly, 'Because if it could the people who own the carpark would have them parked up there.'

Auden finished, 'And they'd have a camera up there to keep an eye on them with, right?'

Klaus said, 'Right.'

Auden said simply to Spencer, 'And since there isn't any camera, then therefore—'

Spencer said, 'That's crazy! Are you telling me the only reason you think a car can't get up onto the roof is because there doesn't seem to be a camera up there? What if somebody *disconnected* the camera?'

Auden gave him a pitying look, 'Then it'd show up on the console as a malfunction.' He was getting the hang of the world of the machine in fast order, 'Right, Klaus?'

'Yes.'

Auden said happily, 'Right.' He leaned over to pat Spencer on the shoulder. Spencer moved away. Auden said explanatorily, 'You have to understand the basis of things like this: things like this work on a *system*. The basis of the system is that it's *organised*. It's a complete sort of *thing*.' (He glanced awkwardly at Klaus and saw blandness in the man's face), 'Isn't that right, Klaus?'

Klaus said, 'Right.' He reached forward and pressed a button that brought up the floor 2 to 3 throughway and then another that displayed the left hand bays at the top and then another that brought up the right, 'And then of course, there's that.'

Auden said, 'What's "that"?'

Klaus said, 'A brick wall. That's another reason the cars can't get up onto the roof.'

Auden said, '—right!'

*

Inside the service elevator on the ground floor level of the hotel The Spaceman held his gloved hand firmly and unyieldingly on the DOOR CLOSE button and waited for the overhead panel above the doors to signal that the elevator was on its way up again.

It came and, with a jerk, the elevator cable took up the slack, the heavy electric motor engaged, and the car rose towards the first floor.

There was an empty food wagon in the elevator, one of its rubber wheels hanging off at an acute angle that suggested that the axle was broken.

The Spaceman moved it carefully to one side to use, if it became necessary, as a barrier or battering ram in his escape.

The elevator rose to the first floor and The Spaceman, his hand on the DOOR CLOSE button, stood very still, listening.

Very vaguely, he could hear piano music.

It was an old sentimental tune from the forties and not one that he recognised.

The little photograph was pushed in against the flame gun clipped to his glove.

He flicked his hand and the little square of tissue wrapped cardboard fluttered slowly to the ground.

*

O'Yee's phone rang. He picked it up and said, 'Detectives' Room,' glanced anxiously in the direction of the door for the second coming of The Slime, saw none, and said, 'Detective Senior Inspector O'Yee.'

A little voice said in Cantonese, 'Daddy, will you say that again while I put my friend Lester on?'

'Patrick, is that you? What the hell are you doing out of school?'

There was a silence and then a sort of kid-breathing sound. Another little voice said in disgust, 'There's no one there. He isn't a real detective at all! I'm going to hit you again!'

O'Yee said, 'Patrick, are you there—?'

Patrick, aged nine, said in a pleading voice, 'Daddy! Say that you're a detective for Lester!'

'Patrick, why aren't you in school?'

Lester said, 'Hullo?'

'I'm a detective.'

There was a pause.

O'Yee drew a long sigh, 'Detective Senior Inspector O'Yee, ma'am. Just give me the facts, ma'am.'

'Wow!' There was a crashing noise as the receiver was fought for in sweaty hands. O'Yee demanded, 'Patrick, why aren't you in school?'

Patrick said back, 'I'm on my way back from lunch. I told Lester that you were going to take our family to the big movies tomorrow night because you're a detective and you know people in the movies and he said he didn't believe me and I—'

O'Yee said quickly, 'As a matter of fact, Patrick, I'm glad you rang because I wanted to talk to you and your mother about that—'

Lester's voice came on dripping with contrite apology, 'I'm really sorry I hit Patrick, Mr O'Yee. He said his Daddy never lied and I didn't believe him because my Daddy tells lies all the time.' He made a snuffling noise, 'My Daddy doesn't love me or Mummy anymore.'

O'Yee said, 'Oh, I'm sorry to hear that, um, um, Lester :.. could you put Patrick :.. '

Lester raised the volume on the snuffling, 'My Daddy just lies and lies and lies. He says he doesn't love us anymore because—'

O'Yee said anxiously, 'Um, maybe you shouldn't be telling me this, um, Lester ... '

Patrick came back onto the line. He said proudly, 'My Daddy doesn't lie, does he Daddy?'

O'Yee said, 'Oh. No. No, no, of course not—'

'Mom was so happy about going she even rang up Grandma and told her you were the cleverest man in the world.' He paused for a moment, 'And Grandma said she didn't believe it.' If extension-listening was any sort of embryonic qualification for spy-work Patrick was well on his way to taking over the CIA at age nine. Patrick said firmly, 'But Mom said you wouldn't lie, not to her, not to me, not to Penelope, not to—'

O'Yee said, 'I get the message.'

Patrick's voice, heavy with menace, said, 'You wouldn't lie to Grandma would you, Daddy?'

The last person who had lied to Grandma had been Grandpa and he had been in a sort of catatonic trance since 1955. If he didn't make the spy business there was always an opening for him in the demanding-money-with-menaces trade. O'Yee said weakly, 'No, I wouldn't lie to anybody.'

There was a struggle at the other end of the line, then Lester came on and asked in a voice thick with emotion, 'You wouldn't be my Daddy too, would you, Mr O'Yee?'

O'Yee said, 'Well, Lester, I—'

Lester said, 'Patrick said I could come with him to the big movies too, didn't you, Patrick?' (Patrick, presumably next to him, said expansively, 'Sure!') 'Is that all right with you, Mr O'Yee?'

That was an easy one, the first break of the day. O'Yee said paternally, 'I'm sorry, Lester, but you'd have to ask Patrick's mother and since I'm getting the tickets today and you've just come back from lunch there just isn't time because you have to get back to school and—'

He was raving. He got control of himself and said, 'Patrick's mother would have to ask you, not Patrick.'

Lester said, 'She did. She asked me and my two sisters and my brother.'

Patrick came back on the line quickly. He said proudly, 'We all know you can do anything. That's what Mom says.' He became businesslike, 'I have to get back to school. Mom says she'll telephone you later and tell you who Lester is for the tickets.' He said happily, 'Bye.'

The line went dead.

Lester? Sure. Why not? His two sisters and one brother? Of course. Certainly. No problem at all. The more the merrier. Happy days. Whoopee. Hoo-ray. 'My Daddy never lies.' Of course, naturally. O'Yee The Untruthful? Never. Impossible. Ha, ha.

In the empty Detectives' Room, O'Yee put the telephone receiver back gently onto its cradle and said, *'AAAGGGHHH!!'*

*

He wasn't colour blind. The roof was empty, flat, deserted, get-up-to-able only via a utility shaft ladder by the conqueror of Everest from the ground floor, but, by God, if there was one thing he wasn't, he wasn't colour blind.

Where the throughway from the third floor would have been if there had been a throughway from the third floor – and there wasn't – there was an enormous generator and air conditioning system. Spencer opened the unlocked door and peered in and saw—

A generator and an air conditioning system.

He looked around on the smooth roof for tyre marks and then for paint spots where the mugger had changed the colour of his Volkswagen and saw—

No tyre marks and no paint spots.

Spencer, the last human being left functioning in a world taken over by the machine, said bitterly, 'When all the possible answers have been eliminated, whatever remains, however impossible, is the solution.'

Spencer went to the edge of the roof and tested his colour vision.

A long way below in Canton Street he could see a traffic light. It was green.

It changed.

Red.

Then it changed back ...

Green again.

Getting down on his hands and knees he looked at the lights upside down just to make sure – just as Holmes would – that it wasn't the fact that his eyes knew the positions of the lights that convinced him he saw the colours, but rather the colours themselves.

Red ... Green ...

He even saw the amber.

Green ... Amber ... Red ...

Red ... Amber ...

From somewhere under him in the carpark itself, he heard the most awful smash as an iron bar collided with a car's plate glass window and, cursing and muttering to himself, he raced back across the roof for the ladder.

*

On the phone O'Yee said desperately to Flick-Knife Fong the Fence, 'Fong? This is O'Yee. Listen, I'll do anything to get a few tickets for the movie premieres tomorrow night. And when I say anything, I mean, anything!'

Flick-Knife Fong said incredulously, 'You're kidding!'

'Anything! You want something done and I'll do it! You want a receiving stolen goods charge quashed, I'm your man!'

Fong thought for a moment, 'No, I'm all right on that at the moment.'

'Dealing in contraband imports?'

'That's fine too.'

'Tax evasion? Robbery with violence? Obscene language? Driving without a licence?'

'Funnily enough, I'm O. K. with all that too.'

'Murder? Kidnapping? Air piracy? Mass poisoning? Selling adulterated food?'

'Not my line.'

'Triad membership? Bribery? Corruption?' O'Yee said with heavy menace, 'You know they're on to you, don't you? You know they're about to pounce, don't you?'

Fong said disbelievingly, 'Nah ... '

'They are. They've got you on the list. You need a friend. Possession of deadly weapons? Keeping explosives without a permit? Treason? Blowing up one of Her Majesty's dockyards?'

Fong said confidently, 'Nah. Nothing.'

'Are you trying to tell me you're clean?'

Flick-Knife Fong said, 'Yeah. I'm going straight.'

'You can't go straight! You're a criminal!'

Flick-Knife Fong said in a holy voice, 'But it's true. At last, I've seen the light.'

'Phoney church donations? Impersonation of a Salvation Army officer? Larceny of church collection plates?'

There was a modest silence.

O'Yee, his voice trailing off into nothingness, said, 'Blasphemy? Possession of the implements of witchcraft? Cockerel buggering? Espionage? Desertion in time of war ... ?'

The clock on the wall of the Detectives' Room, measuring off doom by the moment, went on ticking happily and uncaringly away.

*

Walking towards the elevators in the Palm Court Bar, Kong said breezily, 'What might be a little more to the point, Henry, would be to work out how we might get a peek at some of the new films before the actual premieres. That way we could have a spin-off in the works before the audiences had even finished getting through their first bag of popcorn.'

Wu, still smarting at the thought that true artists starved and he was making a fortune, said, 'Hmm.' He stopped for a moment by a low table to stub out his Corona in a crystal ashtray.

Kong, ever the diplomat, waited. He asked to change the subject, 'What do you think of that publicity stunt of burning the flying saucer?'

Wu, grinding the cigar into dust, said irritably, 'I think it's a pity we didn't think of it first.'

Kong said, 'I guess the street sweeper was some sort of accident.'

He smiled and patted his friend on the shoulder, 'Look at the film business this way, Henry ... '

The doors to the service elevator a little to their left opened with a muffled bang.

Wu, glancing over, said, *'Jesus Christ!'*

'No, it's all been done, Henry ... '

Wu said again, *'Jesus—!'*

The Spaceman stood rock-still inside the open service elevator. Behind the black visor on his helmet he seemed to have no face.

The flame came out of the gun in The Spaceman's hand in a single thundering yellow ball and, setting the floor, the ceiling, and the walls around them on fire, engulfed Henry Wu and Charlie Kong in its swirling lethal centre like a whirlwind.

8

Crouching down over what was left of the two charred bodies in the Palm Court Bar, Doctor Macarthur probed at something with a stainless steel tool and said to himself, *'Fascinating.'* There was a swooshing noise by the service elevator as a Chinese fireman gave a smoking wall panel a blast from a carbon dioxide fire extinguisher. 'It reminds me of some of the reports of injuries sustained by the Buddhist monks who set fire to themselves in the street during the Viet Nam war.' The floor was ankle deep in vile smelling foam and liquid from the overhead sprinkler system. He took away the probe and stood up, nodding for the waiting ambulancemen to come over from the main elevators with their plastic body bags, 'Fascinating. Really quite fascinating.'

Next to Feiffer and Lee, the Chief Fire Safety Officer of Hong Bay, a heavy set khaki uniformed Australian named George Bell, watched as the fireman doused the last whisps of blue smoke on the wall with the extinguisher. The fireman stepped back to admire his work and Bell said in Cantonese, 'Very good. You've put it out. Now do it again to make sure it bloodywell stays out!' He waited until the swooshing started again and asked Feiffer, 'Who were they?'

Anthony Lam and Teddy Wong were standing a little way off near the piano. The lady piano player stood next to them, looking away.

Feiffer said with his eyes still on Lam and Wong, 'According to Lam it looks like they were a couple of Chinese-American film producers based in the Philippines.' He glanced down at his open notebook and turned a page, 'Kong and Wu. They deposited some stuff in the office safe so Lam remembers them. He thinks they made cheap follow-up films based on whatever was the big box-office success of the moment.'

Bell said with sudden feeling, 'It looks to me like the big box-office success of the moment is your fucking spaceman!' He indicated a soaked, black rag near the windows that had once been a twelve foot wide double drape curtain, 'All the stuff in this bloody place is cheap quality high-burn man-made nylon. That stink you can smell is the special liquid from the sprinklers you're supposed to use these days to put it out if it catches fire. The sprinkler tank only holds so much special liquid, so if your little spaceman decides the next time to really set the place on fire we won't be standing around discussing bloody Buddhist monks' – that was intended for Macarthur – 'We'll be standing around discussing what a nice place Hong Kong used to be before it got burned to the ground.' Bell said with a hard look on his face, 'I was in Viet Nam, Doctor Macarthur, and I didn't think burning bloody Buddhists were in the least bloody fascinating!'

Macarthur took out a cigarette and put it into his mouth. Going a little red, he said, 'I mean, strictly in the medical sense.'

Bell snapped, 'Put out that bloody cigarette!'

Feiffer touched Bell on the shoulder and moved to stand between him and Macarthur. He asked Macarthur, 'Is it definitely petrol again?'

Bell said, 'Yes.' He glanced over at Lam and, still glaring at Macarthur, said quietly to Feiffer, 'That manager character—what's his name?'

'Lam.'

'Lam. He's a bloody nut-case.' (The two ambulancemen came up from the elevator opening their plastic body bags and glanced at Bell for permission. Bell said, 'Yeah, get on with it.') 'When I got here with my boys I tried to get him to tell me where the sprinkler turn-off valve was. It took me at least five minutes to stop him from having a bloody nervous break-down on the spot. If it hadn't been for his mate there – (Feiffer said, 'Teddy Wong') – I'd be still ringing up the Brigade's central computer to get a sprinkler valve location print-out. I asked him if he saw who did it and he shouted at me that he got messages on smoke and water. He's a bloody nut.'

Feiffer nodded. He looked over at Lam and saw the man had tears running down his cheeks. Teddy Wong was absently patting him on the arm. Lam turned for a moment to look at the lady by the piano, but she – with a sudden hard look in her eyes – looked away and ignored him. Feiffer asked Macarthur, 'Is there anything you can tell from the bodies that we didn't already know from the street sweeper?'

'No.' Macarthur took the unlit cigarette out of his mouth, looked at Bell thoughtfully, then stuck it back in his mouth again, still unlit.

Bell asked, 'Any witnesses?'

'The lady piano player.' Feiffer glanced at her. 'One of my Constables took an on-the-spot statement from her, but I may get a little more from her after the bodies have been taken away.' He was interested in the way she seemed to be reacting to Lam and Teddy Wong. Teddy Wong, on several occasions, had turned to her and, in a combination of sympathy and embarrassment, smiled encouragingly at her. She had smiled back and then, once Wong's back was again turned, her eyes had strayed to Lam and become narrowed with contempt. Feiffer said, 'I doubt whether Lam can contribute much more than real or imagined paranoia at the moment.' He said to George Bell, 'The other man with him – Wong – is with an insurance company. Maybe you could use that as an excuse and take them both off on a tour of the hotel's fire doors or something.'

'I was going to anyway. Apart from anything else, this sprinkler system has got to be refilled at the main tank and I want to make sure somebody promises to do it.' He said to a Chinese senior fire officer by the fireman with the extinguisher, 'Mr Chang, it might be an idea considering the design of this place to go downstairs to the foyer and get the switchboard to check with the other floors that the fumes and smoke were extruded via the emergency outlet and not straight into the airconditioning system.' He said to Feiffer with the slightest trace of professional pique, 'I was going to check the fire doors anyway.'

'Thanks.'

Macarthur, lighting his cigarette from his Zippo lighter, said with a relieved exhalation of pungent blue smoke. 'Is there anything else I can do?'

Feiffer shook his head.

Bell, watching the two body bags being loaded into the elevator, sniffed. He could still vaguely smell the petrol under the heavier cloying stink of burned nylon and human flesh.

Bell, breathing hard, said with sudden irritation, his mind travelling back to something he had seen in a Saigon street that seemed an age ago, 'You can do something for me.'

The Buddhist monk had used a Zippo. He had flipped the cover open, flicked it again, harder.

Macarthur said with an accommodating smile, 'Sure, what's that?'

Bell snarled, 'You can put out that bloody cigarette for a start!' He railed at Macarthur with more intensity than he had intended, 'You stupid, dumb, bloody bastard, don't you know the smell of bloody petrol when it's all around you?'

Once a human body doused in that stuff caught fire, it was impossible to put it out. In Saigon that morning, he had tried it first with his Army camouflage jacket and then with his bare hands. Sometimes at night, he still remembered the monk's face in the flames.

It had seemed to be smiling at him.

*

426. The code number of a Fighting Leader of a Triad secret society.

426. The Red Pole or Hung Kwan, ranked number two or three. Feiffer turned the little photograph over in his hand, careful not to put his fingers on either the front or the back of the glossy little square of cardboard.

Detective Chief Inspector Harry Feiffer ... If the Chinese secret societies needed a cast-list then they had gone badly down the hill in the last few years.

426 ...

Messages on smoke and water ...

He waited until Bell and Macarthur went towards the service stairs with Lam and Wong and, as the elderly European lady sat down again at her piano and, for something to do, ran her fingers across the keys in a series of tuneless exercises, slipped the photograph into a little glassine envelope in his pocket and went over towards her.

*

On the third floor, Auden shouted breathlessly at Spencer, 'I saw it! I actually saw it going away after the mugging!' There was a red Toyota in one of the left hand bays, the middle aged Chinese driver standing next to his shattered off-side window picking glass out of his suit and looking dazed. Auden said, 'I was scanning the entire complex and then—Klaus was telling me about the doppler system and then we—I pressed up the third floor and I ran up here—' He looked at the dazed man by the Toyota, 'And it didn't pass me going down!' He demanded, 'Where the hell were you?'

'I came down from the roof. The ladder only goes from the roof to the ground. I had to come up here along the throughways.' Spencer said, 'It didn't pass me either.'

'Then it must have gone *up!*' The brick wall was in front of him. Auden said, 'It has to have passed through solid brick!'

'No. I heard the bang. If it had come straight up onto the roof I would have seen it.'

Auden said, baffled, 'It can't go up onto the roof, can it?' 'No.'

'Then where the hell's it gone?' Auden said, 'It's gone.'

The Toyota man suddenly seemed to realise what had happened to his brand new Toyota and said, 'Oh, NO!' There had been an expensive Hasselblad camera on the off-side seat next to him. He evidently realised what had happened to that too, and yelled, 'Oh, NO! NO! NO!' He focussed on Auden and stabbed out an accusing finger at him.

Spencer said, 'We're police.'

'Then get after it!' The Toyota man said, 'It was a Volkswagen kombi van! It was yellow!' He pointed in the direction of the throughway down to the next floor, 'It went that way!'

Auden said, 'No, it couldn't have—'

'It did! I saw it go!'

Auden said again, 'No ... ' He grabbed Spencer by both shoulders and shook him. Auden said with his eyes rolling around in his head, 'Dammit, Bill, I saw it escaping on the screen!' He yelled back to the advancing Toyota driver, 'You're lying! I saw it! It wasn't yellow! It was *white!*' He thought in one terrible instant that if the Toyota driver said, 'Yellow,' at the very least, he might be losing his mind.

The Toyota man said emphatically, 'I saw it in my rear view mirror when it stopped!' He demanded suspiciously as a large piece of cobwebbed smashed windscreen dislodged itself from his coat and fell to the cement floor with a bang, 'What the hell's the matter with you goddamned cops anyway? Are you all *colour-blind* or something? It was yellow!'

*

In the cells, The Green Slime drew a deep breath and bawled out at the top of his lungs, 'You dirty lousy stinking half-caste Eurasian pig-cop! Come down here and beat me up—I dare you! Pig-cop! You lousy—'

He was growing desperate. He reached out through the grille with the second pick and tension tool he had made from matchsticks and undid the lock, opened the cell door and, sweating profusely in fear as the light from the corridor window told him the time was getting away fast, wondered what, for the sake of his wife and family, he should do.

He yelled out without conviction, 'You dirty cop!' got no reply, and, putting his webbed palm to his head, went back inside the cell and wrung his hands together until they hurt.

*

The elderly lady at the piano wore pearls and a twin set. She had tears in her eyes. Her fingers moved over the piano keys and touched gently at the introduction to *Together*. She put out her hand and Feiffer took it.

The elderly woman smiled at him, 'I'm Mrs Coates.' The line of her mouth seemed tired and somehow very disappointed. She touched at her throat and gave Feiffer a faint, half smile, 'My stage name is Carole. "Carole Plays

For You In The Palm Court Bar." Have you ever—
"Carole Entertains On The—" '

The smell of the burned nylon and flesh was still very strong in the room. Feiffer nodded.

Carole touched at the keys again. 'My husband and I both used to be in show business together—in Simla.' She asked, 'Have you ever heard of Simla?'

'It was a sort of mountain resort in India during the Raj, wasn't it?'

'Yes! That's exactly what it was.' She seemed very pleased, 'That's exactly what it was. It was—'

Feiffer asked, 'Did you see him? The man with the gun?'

Carole said, 'I was playing for the guests. For the two Chinese who were—' She looked down at the piano, 'My husband and I, we used to run a cinema in Delhi. I was the accompanist to some of the old silent films, the organist—' Her hands were very lined and old. She rubbed her thumbs over the tips of her fingers and looked down at the keyboard. 'Did you ever go to a cinema where— This used to be a really nice hotel once. Before the Singapore owners took it over. Once, it used to be where nice people came and—' She asked Feiffer, 'Did you ever come here with—with your wife or your lady friend or—'

'I used to come here sometimes with my parents.'

'Oh.' There was a row of empty chairs to one side of the piano. Carole said, 'In the old days my friends used to come here for afternoon tea and sit with me and talk. The old management used to give them free cakes and—' She made a sniffing sound and wiped at her eyes, 'They're going to send me downstairs to the foyer now. Now that the Palm Court is gone—that man Lam will replace it with glass and stainless steel and gramophone music and—' Carole said, 'We used to show such lovely films in the old days. We had all the Carole Lombard films' - she paused, but Feiffer said nothing - 'And all the Veronica

73

Lake films and the—' She looked down at the keys, 'All our old friends went back home after Independence and the Indians didn't want to see films like that so we—'

Feiffer said gently, 'You're the only witness I have, Mrs Coates.'

There was a bitter smile on Carole's face. 'So we tried to set up a cinema in Shanghai, but then the Communists came in. My husband—he thought we should have gone home to England there and then, but I—' She said in a whisper, 'You can't set up a cinema here because of the Triads. They demand enormous extortion and a little private cinema just can't cope with it.' She said thickly, on the edge of crying, 'All my friends used to come here to sit with me for afternoon tea—' She touched at the cover of the grand piano, 'The management will move me down to the foyer now and—'

Feiffer asked, 'Are there any Triad men in the hotel?'

'I don't know. They don't care about me.'

'Among the waiters or—'

'No.' Carole said softly, 'The doors on the service elevator just opened and then one of the Chinese men said a blasphemy and then, a moment later—' She said in a choked voice, 'I heard screaming like that in Shanghai when the Communists burned our little cinema down with everybody inside because we were showing a film about—' Carole said, 'It wasn't a spaceman. It was a man dressed in a firefighting suit.'

'Are you sure?'

Carole said, 'Yes.' She looked down at the piano, 'I should be sorry for the two men. One of them seemed nice. He—' She looked up at the ceiling, 'When the sprinkler system started I thought it might fall onto my piano and ruin it.' She put her hand into a fist and put it against her mouth, 'It's mine, you see, all I have left from when—I thought the sprinklers might have ruined it. It's insured for a lot of money.' She looked at the row of empty chairs that looked like they had not been sat on for a very long time, 'It's all I have left.'

Feiffer nodded.

Carole said, 'It's all I have left. All I've got for all those years ... when my husband was alive. From Simla and Delhi, and Shanghai and—'

Feiffer touched her hand. 'It isn't damaged. The sprinklers didn't go off in this part of the room.'

'No.'

'Are you sure it was a firefighting suit? Asbestos?'

'Yes. It had a soft helmet and—' Carole said, blinking, 'I saw them in Shanghai.' She asked, 'Have you ever been to—'

'Yes. My father was in Shanghai before the war.'

'Really?' Carole said, 'Really? Do you remember any of it? Bubbling Well Road, and Sincere's the big shop in—and The Bund and—and all the ships—'

'I can remember Bubbling Well Road. My father's company had its offices there.'

'Truly?' She seemed to be almost pleading with him. She said desperately, 'They'll move me down into the foyer now and then as soon as they can—as soon as the awful common people who come here now complain they want modern gramophone music, they'll—'

Feiffer touched her hand again, 'The piano isn't damaged. It's all right.' He wondered whether the tears in her eyes were due more to partial blindness. He asked gently, 'How old are you, Carole?'

'I'm almost seventy five.'

Feiffer said, 'The piano's all right, I promise you. I can't see a mark on it.'

'It's insured for a lot of money. It's all I have left.' Carole said with tears suddenly rolling down her cheeks, 'Oh God damn it all, if he had burned it—'

'I know.'

Carole protested at the unfairness of it all, 'Oh God, if he had burned it I could have claimed the money on it and gone home to England!' She crashed both her fists down on the keys cacophonously and shouted to the burned-out room in a high, old lady's voice, 'It's not right! First Independence and then the Communists and then the Triads, and now this!' She grasped Feiffer's hand hard, 'You understand, don't you? Now they're going to move me into the foyer and all I want to do is go home to England and die!'

She squeezed Feiffer's hand until it hurt. The elderly woman named after a film star long dead said with tears coursing down her cheeks, 'He could have burned it, couldn't he? He could have burned it and it would have cost him nothing.' She said desperately to the unfairness of it all, 'Isn't there anybody – *anybody* who can understand?'

*

The barman at The Lucky Dime had the information that Hot Time Alice Ping wasn't in. Hot Time Alice Ping, he told O'Yee over the phone (it took surprisingly few threats to get it out of him) was at Wan Chai Station for the third time that day bailing out her whores.

The barman asked, 'Premiere tickets? You're asking me if I've got any movie premiere tickets?' The barman said, 'If I had any movie premiere tickets with the people who run this place I wouldn't have any hands.' The barman said, 'Listen.' There was a cracking noise at the other end of the phone. The barman said, 'That was me cracking my knuckles. Knuckles I happen to have because I still happen to have hands. If I had movie premiere tickets I hadn't told the people who run this place about the only noise I might be able to make is a sort of bandaged stump sound.'

'All right, so you haven't got any tickets.'

The barman said, 'Right first time. You've got it. This is Two Handed Ling telling you he hasn't got any tickets.

You hear Two Handed Ling telling you that with his voice because Two Handed Ling still has a head connected to his body with which to tell you he hasn't—'

'Forget I asked!'

'I will.' The barman said, 'Two Handed Still Headed Ling has a future in which to forget that, in the past ... '

*

On the third floor of the carpark, Spencer took Auden gently across to the street side to show him the traffic lights.

There was a building in the way and they couldn't be seen.

Spencer said, 'That's odd. I could see them from the roof.' Mustering enthusiasm, he said to Auden cheeringly, 'Listen, I've got an idea. Let's consider the whole thing again another way right from the beginning ...'

*

It was 2 p.m. and Constables Lee and Sun were getting bored with the million dollars and beginning to find themselves straying away for the exercise.

The Spaceman was watching them.

He looked at the time.

9

In the Detectives' Room, Feiffer took back the photograph from O'Yee and said, 'It was taken about a week ago from the foyer of the hotel.' He saw O'Yee's surprised look, 'That's part of the Hong Bay branch of the Bank of America in the background. It's opposite the hotel, I paced out the approximate distance judging by the size of the face in the photo and it was taken from either just outside or just inside the hotel foyer. And the reason I happen to know it was taken last week is that being poor but honest I only happen to have two suits and the one in the picture is at the cleaners.' You could just make out the window of the bank and a series of cards and advertisements stuck on it. Feiffer said, 'The exchange rates on the window are last Thursday's.' O'Yee had a copy of the register of the hotel guests on his desk. 'Do you recognise any of the names?'

'I recognise the names of half a dozen people who make science fiction movies.' O'Yee glanced down the list for the third time, 'Yamamoto, Onuki, Ishimaru, Fernandez, Wing, Mukherjee – most of these people seem to be either Japanese or Philippino or Chinese-American.' He turned the page over and looked down a list of the names of the hotel employees, 'If there's anyone working there of even minor importance I don't know him. Have you sent the list to the Anti-Triad Bureau?'

'They're ringing me when they've run it through their files.' Feiffer said, 'The obvious thing is to search the hotel, but since there are over five hundred rooms—'

'We could probably get in some help—some special Constables or—'

'To look for what? A firefighting outfit that can be folded up into a small briefcase? The way this character seems to be able to appear and disappear at will it's hardly likely he'll have left it around for anyone to find. As for the gun, if he can conceal it in his hand it's about the size of a small revolver. I walked through a few of the hotel corridors and in the course of four floors I didn't see one other human being. All the potential witnesses are out in the streets dressed up as space monsters.' Feiffer put the photograph in his Out tray to be taken around to the Fingerprint Section, 'Unless he's got an accomplice, The Spaceman took this photograph himself, which means he was here at least a week before the Congress started.' He said before O'Yee could ask, 'And before you ask, the photograph is Polaroid, so I'm spared the dubious pleasure of going around the two thousand or so camera shops in the Colony asking who developed it.' He lit a cigarette, looking tired, and said bitterly, 'I seem to be spared quite a lot on this one: all I've got to do is hang around until he decides to incinerate someone else.'

'Or gets what he's after.'

'Which is?'

O'Yee shrugged. 'The million dollars?'

'Then why not just go in and get it?'

'Maybe because of the insurance aspect.'

'The insurance aspect is a figment of Lam's over-active imagination. If The Spaceman wanted to burn the hotel down he certainly could have done it without going around blowing up flying saucers and street sweepers and film producers in a fin-de-siècle Palm Court.' Feiffer said irritably, 'It's only in Big Job movies the bad guys enter banks dressed as nuns carrying anti-tank guns. In the real world, people who want to rob banks or hotels just stroll in with handkerchiefs over their faces and Saturday Night Specials in their hands and yell "Stick 'em up." Even bloody psychos don't dress up because they're too busy being bloody psychos. And they don't go in for ray guns—they go in for knives and axes.' His phone rang and he picked it up quickly and said, 'Yes?'

It was Chief Inspector Roberts from the Companies Squad. Roberts said, 'Harry, we've just heard back from the Singapore police and all this stuff about the owners of the Empress of India hotel not wanting to make a profit is a load of horseshit. For a start, the company's registered in Hong Kong and any profits they might make here wouldn't count one iota against their Singapore tax liability.' Roberts asked curiously, 'Who told you all that anyway?'

'A man who gets messages on his cigarettes.'

'Then his cigarettes have got something a bit stronger than tobacco in them. The people who own the hotel want a loss about as much as I want leprosy. According to the Singapore Companies Squad they've just spent a small fortune modernising the place. Lam's under a lot of pressure all right, but it's pressure to *make* money. Some of the other enterprises the consortium have invested in in Singapore aren't doing too well and the last thing they want is to see the Hong Kong money flow drop. As for them wanting the place burned to the ground for the insurance, forget it.' Roberts paused for a moment, 'The Singapore cops said they didn't want to make too much of what I'm about to tell you because it isn't their job to start crisis-of-confidence rumours, but if Lam has lost his marbles then the entire Singapore consortium is in deep trouble unless they can replace him pretty quick smart. Evidently he's a real winner because he's got the common touch or something—'

Feiffer said, 'Yeah. His main asset is that he can't read French menus either.'

'Whatever.' Roberts said, 'The million dollars may be fully insured all right, but the hotel isn't. If your Spaceman is in the arson-for-profit trade, then the hotel owners aren't his employers. They'd get back about one cent in the dollar.' Roberts said quickly, 'And before you therefore leap to the obvious line that The Spaceman is some sort of saboteur from other hotels in the Colony jealous at the Empress of India's full rooms, let me tell you that there isn't an empty two to four star room in the entire place. All the other major hotels have had a couple of hundred enquiries each from guests staying at the Empress who don't care for the notion of being the next on the waste-disposal list, *but not one of the hotels has been able to accommodate a single one of them.*' Roberts said, 'All this is a free service from your otherwise totally idle Companies Squad. The nice thing about Sci Fi Congresses is that nobody bothers going to work during them so the embezzlers and con men are all out at the movies.' He asked breezily, 'Anything else I can do for you?'

'Is there any truth in Lam's idea that there's someone else waiting in the wings to take over if he fails?'

'Possibly, but I don't know who. I suppose it'd only be sensible if Lam is showing signs of going bananas.'

Feiffer asked, 'What about the Foochow Insurance Company? Teddy Wong's outfit. The ones who insured the million dollars?'

'All I know is that they're a small, one man firm and that if Wong took a straight do-or-die risk on a cool million then he probably laid most of it off over three or four bigger companies. We did a survey on some of the small insurance firms a few years back, but I don't recall that the Foochow was in business then. Wong's only been in insurance briefly. Before that he used to be—' Roberts hesitated and said, 'Um ... '

Feiffer waited.

'He made his pile and went into insurance. Whether or

not Foochow is solid I'm not sure.' He said, 'Hang on a minute.' (He said to someone in the background, 'Oh, yeah? Thanks, Alan.') He came back on the line, 'Alan Cheung here says he thinks Tax may be still after him. He doubts whether any of the big Hong Kong insurance companies would deal with him.' Roberts asked, 'Is that of any real interest to anyone except him?'

'Not unless he happens to have been in the arson business before he went into insurance.'

'No.' Roberts said, 'As a matter of fact, he was with—' He said suddenly, 'I remember the name: it was The Orient Dragon, in Nathan Road. It went bust when the owners decided to put their dollars on short term profitable loan American dollars and the Americans decided to put the dollar on temporary long-term inflationary worthlessness.' Roberts said, 'He ran the place all right too, from what I heard. A Canadian friend of mine stayed there for a bit and said it was all up-to-date, comfortable, and about as common as bloody dirt, just like the Empress of India is now.' Roberts said philosophically, 'Do you think it could be the influence of Socialism, Harry, all this creeping erosion of—'

Feiffer said, 'It was a hotel?'

'The Orient Dragon? Sure. I just said so.'

'And Teddy Wong was—' Feiffer looked down at the photograph and then over to O'Yee.

Roberts said, 'Teddy Wong was the manager.'

O'Yee had come over from his desk. He took the little photograph from Feiffer's tray and turned it in its glassine envelope to catch the light.

There were two faint pencil lines drawn in over the face in the picture, intersecting like—

Roberts said, 'Listen, Harry, if you want a hand over there—'

—like a target seen through the lens of the telescopic sights of a high powered rifle.

O'Yee turned the photograph over.

Detective Chief Inspector Harry Feiffer, Yellowthread Street Station, Hong Bay.

426.

O'Yee heard Constable Yan coming down the corridor from the charge room whistling to himself and he wrenched open the door of the Detectives' Room and shouted at him to take the photograph over to the Triad Bureau Central office as fast as the crowds in the streets outside would let him go.

*

By the smashed pylon in the left hand bays of the second floor, Spencer picked up a few shards of broken neon tube and held them out in his hand for Auden to identify.

Spencer said, 'They're white, aren't they?'

Auden nodded.

'So you're not colour blind.' Spencer said, 'Look, the first six victims of the mugger on the second floor saw his Volkswagen as yellow, right? They saw it in their rear view mirrors as it drove past. Right?'

Auden scowled at him and, against his better judgement, nodded.

'Then the next victim on the third floor – in the right hand parking bays – said it was blue.' There was a blue Renault 6 parked a few bays away from the pylon and Spencer pointed at it and said, 'Blue. Right? Do you see that as blue?'

'Of course I see it as bloody blue!'

Spencer reached out to pat him on the shoulder to pacify him. Auden moved away. 'Then the next victim – the last – said it was yellow again.'

Auden made a sort of an about-to-spring Bengal tiger noise.

Spencer said, 'And then you—seeing it going away on

the TV screen, on the third floor: the same vehicle in the same attack, number eight—'

Auden said, 'I know which bloody one it was! I may not be able to bloody see straight, but I can bloody count!'

'You said it was white.'

'It was bloody white! That bloody television in the ticket booth is in colour! If it was in bloody black and white I might not have seen it as white, but it isn't! It's in colour! And the back of that bloody Kraut wagon was white!'

Spencer said, nodding, 'Right.'

'What the hell do you mean, "Right"?' Auden took a step forward, 'Listen, Spencer, if this is another one of your bloody Sherlock Holmes tricks—'

Spencer said, 'Sherlock Holmes didn't have to deal with machines! He worked things out for himself!'

'He could bloodywell afford to! He didn't have bloody German kombi vans running all around the place changing their spots like bloody leopards!'

Spencer said helpfully, 'Actually, the point of that expression is that leopards *don't* change their—'

Auden said warningly, 'Don't try to be funny! I'm warning you, just don't try to be—'

'I'm not.' Spencer picked up yet another piece of smashed neon tube (Auden said, 'It's bloody white. All right?') and said mildly, 'Listen, Phil, machines are only there to help you see reality *more clearly.*' (Auden gave him a quizzical look) 'There's no question that they actually change reality.' Spencer said, 'Esse est percipi—'

Auden said, 'What the hell does that mean?'

'That means that leopards don't change their spots.' Spencer was thinking hard, 'Maybe it means that all those other people saw the van as yellow for the reason that it was yellow and the seventh victim, he saw it as blue because—'

Auden looked interested.

Spencer said, '—because it *was* blue.'

Auden said, 'WHAT—?!'

'And you, you saw it as white because—'

'Because, as well as being bloody yellow and bloody blue it was also bloody white! Right?'

Spencer said, *'Right!'*

'Are you out of your goddamned mind?'

Spencer gave him his Holmes look. 'All right, how many sides does a basically rectangular Volkswagen kombi van have?'

Auden said, 'Four.' He said, 'Are you telling me that—' He looked at the smashed neon tube on the ground and then at the shards in Spencer's hand, 'Are you telling me that because the van was stopped one way on the third floor and another on the second it changed from— *It had two colours on the third floor,* not one! Blue and bloody yellow!'

Spencer smiled, 'One in the left hand side bays and one in the right. Just as if it was pointing in different directions each time for a quick escape and different sides of it were seen by different people.'

Auden said, 'And, and— By God, Bill, when I saw it on the TV screen I only saw the back of it!'

Spencer nodded sagely, 'Right.'

'It's yellow on one side and blue on the other and—*and the back of it is white!'* Auden said, impressed beyond words, 'By God, Bill, that's bloody brilliant! You've solved it! I'll never say a word against bloody Sherlock Holmes again so long as I live!' Auden said in a lather of admiration, 'By God, I'll buy you a bloody Deerstalker hat for your birthday! And a calabash pipe!' He asked respectfully, carefully, ready to follow The Great Detective's merest syllable, 'O.K., now we know it's still in the carpark somewhere so you can tell me where it is and you just rest now and leave it to me and I'll—'

Spencer glanced down at the shards and shrugged, 'Well, actually, Phil, to be honest, that part of it – I mean,

where it is – ' Spencer said, 'I haven't actually worked that
bit out yet—'

Auden said, 'WHAT—?!'

*

On the other end of the phone, Mr Chang, the Deputy
Chief Fire Safety Officer for Hong Bay, said in English,
'No, sir, I'm afraid Mr Bell isn't here at the moment. Can I
do anything?'

'This is Detective Chief Inspector Feiffer from Yellowthread Street. (Chang said, 'Oh, yes, I saw you at the
hotel.') I've had information that the outfit the so-called
Spaceman is wearing might be some sort of lightweight
firefighting outfit.'

There was a pause and then Mr Chang said, 'No, sir.
There's a drawing of it on the front page of the newspaper
in front of me. You wouldn't wear a glass bubble helmet if
you were—'

'It isn't a glass bubble helmet. The sweeper who survived
this morning couldn't do much better than to say The
Spaceman didn't look like the ones he'd seen on the
movies. I've now spoken to a more reliable witness who
says the helmet was soft. She claims to have seen outfits
like it before.'

There was a moment's silence, then Chang said, 'I
suppose it would figure if The Spaceman knew the carpets
and curtains in the hotel were made of nylon. If anyone
was stupid enough to throw water on them while he still
had the gun going without protection the explosion might
well burn his head off along with everyone else's.'

'I want to know where someone would get something
like that in Hong Kong and what they're made of and who
makes them.'

'They're made of asbestos and flame-proof Plexiglas for
the faceplate.' Chang said, 'Not the sort of thing you go

into a shop and buy. They're imported on permit. Some factories have got them. And of course the Airport.' He asked, 'Did the suit have any sort of marking on it?'

'No.'

'Then it wouldn't have been from a factory or the Airport. It's a bye-law here that fixed premises suits have to be marked clearly and indelibly so they can be taken in and checked once a year by the Government Testing Laboratories.' Chang said informatively, 'You know, to make sure they haven't perished or someone's cut a section from the leg to put over his pot-plate in the canteen or something.'

'What about the Army then or the—'

'No. All the military have standard British forces issue suits. They're extremely heavy duty for fires in ammunition stores or burning aircraft and tanks. Out in the open you couldn't even move in one of them. And they're kept by the Emergency Services people at the various depots under strong security. And they're checked, I know for a fact, at least once a day.' He said before Feiffer could ask, 'And as for ours – for the Fire Brigade's – you'd have more chance of stealing the Crown Jewels from the Tower of London.'

'Are yours the right sort?'

'You haven't told me exactly what sort you—'

Feiffer said, 'You just told me: lightweight, unmarked, with a soft helmet and a Plexiglas faceplate.'

'They're the right sort.' Chang said reasonably, 'But we haven't lost any.'

'You don't have any in other stations?'

'No. They're all kept here. We're the Hong Kong Central Depot.' Chang said, 'As a matter of fact, I was just on my way out when you rang and I'm taking this call from the Stores Issue Room itself. I can see the shelves with the suits packed up on them.' He read off, 'Shelves one to twenty five, twenty five to fifty, fifty to seventy two ... three ... four ... ' He said, 'Yes, they're all here.'

'All seventy four of them?'

'Yes.'

Feiffer said again, 'Seventy four?'

'Seventy five with Mr Bell's suit. Mr Bell's one isn't kept here.'

'No?' Feiffer asked, 'Why is that?'

'Mr Bell is the Chief Fire Safety Officer, Mr Feiffer. He attends fires independently of Brigade. Obviously if fire fighting suits were needed Brigade might not have brought one for him.' He said definitely, 'In fact, they wouldn't have. We only issue them on a one-for-one basis.'

'Where does Mr Bell keep his suit if it's not in Stores?'

'In his car.' Chang said helpfully, 'They fold up. You could keep it in an ordinary briefcase if you wanted to.' There was a silence at the other end of the line and Mr Chang said, 'Mr Feiffer, are you still there?'

'Does Mr Bell keep his in a briefcase?'

'Yes. It's usual Brigade practice.'

'Where is he now? Is he out on a job?'

'Officially, I don't know that either. Mr Bell does pretty much what he likes.' Mr Chang made a sort of tentative chuckling sound, 'But just between you and me, he sort of vaguely suggested that after he'd had another look around the Empress of India hotel he might well, accidentally find himself out of touch for a few hours. He said there was a movie on at the Roxy he wanted to see.'

There was another silence, longer, and then Feiffer said very quietly, 'Really? What movie was that?'

Chang said, 'The Towering Inferno. Mr Bell said he'd missed it the first time around.' Again, there was that silence.

Mr Chang said in vague alarm, 'Mr Feiffer, have I said something wrong or something? It's perfectly all right. Mr Bell often takes time off when there's something else he wants to do. It's just one of the senior officers' perks. It's perfectly all right.' Mr Chang said anxiously, 'Honestly, Mr Feiffer, he always makes up the time he loses.'

⁕

At the money, Constable Lee watched the fourteenth scantily-clad destined-to-be-clutched-in-the-monster's-arms girl parade the length of the foyer in search of admiration, and said to Sun with a sigh, 'I'm getting sick of this.' He looked at one of the girls pause to adjust what little there was to adjust on a diaphanous get-up the size of a baby's nightdress, turned his thoughts to the million dollars, found even that failed to excite him and said with another sigh, 'I must be getting old.'

Constable Sun nodded. Diaphanous ladies, mounds of greenbacks and Spacemen notwithstanding, he had taken to occupying himself by counting the number of eyelets the laces went through in his shoes. Constable Sun said, 'I even wish I was at home listening to my wife or shouting at the kids.' There was a flash of brown thigh from one of the nymphs, 'That reminds me: I promised my wife to stop off at the markets and buy a couple of nice fish for her brother's big birthday meal.' He saw someone in uniform pass behind the million dollar watchers and called out in English as the man cleared them and made for the service stairs down to the basement, 'How are you, Mr Bell?' He saw Bell pause and try to place him, 'Constable Sun, sir, from Yellowthread Street.'

Bell nodded.

Constable Lee said smiling, 'Lee, sir.' He gave a little half salute as Bell smiled at him.

Sun said, 'Hard working guy, that, for a European.'

He went back to counting the eyelets in his shoes as Bell went downstairs towards the hotel basement.

It was three o'clock in the afternoon.

Bored beyond words, Constable Sun yawned mightily and thought of nice fish for his wife's brother's birthday celebration.

10

On the phone Deputy Superintendent Ashwood made a snorting noise. Ashwood said easily, 'I once got a birthday card signed Raquel Walsh, but that wasn't genuine either.' He had one of those Australian accents that put the end of a sentence into the higher nasal registers and turned it into a question, 'The Triads don't sign target pictures with their numbers or anything else.' He paused for a moment. 'And they certainly don't kill cops.'

Feiffer said irritably, 'I didn't say it was from the Triads, what I said was that I thought someone wanted me to *think* it was from the Triads.'

'Then you've answered your own question.' Ashwood said, 'The number 426, as you probably know, is the code for a Hung Kwan—a Triad fighting leader. Apart from anything else, he isn't the one who'd be concerned with targetting: he'd be more likely to supply the knives or choppers for a 49 – an ordinary member – to do the targetting.' Ashwood said on only too familiar ground, 'When the Triads decide to knock someone off they don't stand around taking pictures, they just do it.'

'You don't know anything about Triad involvement in the Empress of India hotel?'

'Why do you ask that?'

'Because that's where I found the photograph.'

Ashwood said too quickly, 'No.'

'That's funny, because I was under the impression the

Anti-Triad Bureau had the place under surveillance.'

'Who the hell told you that?'

Feiffer said sweetly, 'No one, as a matter of fact, but it wasn't a bad guess, was it?' He demanded, 'Where's the authorisation from my Station so you people can go working on our patch? I don't seem to have one.'

'It doesn't concern your Station. It had nothing to do with local matters.' Ashwood said with a sneaking admiration, 'Is that how you do your best frames? Ask the punters trick questions?'

'No, normally we just beat a confession out of them.'

Ashwood snorted. His tone became brisk. 'Listen, Harry, you know as well as I do that the Triads are big business now. All the street corner local Station Tong War type stuff is just old meat cleavers as far as they're concerned. They're organised like the Mafia these days—corporately.'

'And they're buying into the hotel business?'

Ashwood said, 'Better stick to beatings-up if that's your best second trick question. As far as we know, the Empress of India is owned by a group in Singapore who are in more need of accountants than Triads. No, what we were doing watching the Empress concerned another matter entirely.'

'Like what?'

Ashwood paused for a moment, 'Like, the Yakuza.'

'The Japanese Mafia?'

'If you want to call them that, yes. They came in a few days before this science fiction congress nonsense got started, made a contact at the hotel and then – I must admit, not without a little prod from us – left again.' He said dismissively, 'It was purely a Bureau matter. For all I know, they might have been over here on your manor for nothing more dastardly than autograph-collecting. In any event, they've gone now.'

'Who did they see at the hotel?'

'Just a businessman.'

Feiffer said, 'Named?'

'Why do you want to know?'

'I want to know because three people have been murdered in and around that hotel! And that is a local Station matter!'

'Yeah, O.K., O.K.' Ashwood said, 'I know. I saw George Bell earlier this morning and he mentioned that—'

'You know Bell?' Feiffer said abruptly, 'That's right, you're an Australian too, aren't you?'

'Yep, Ashwood the loud-mouthed Ocker. That's me all right.'

'No need to get touchy.'

'Touchy? Me?' Ashwood said without a great deal of humour in his voice, 'Listen, when I start doing "touchy" you'll know about it. Yes, I know George.' He paused for a moment, 'As a matter of fact we were in Viet Nam together, in Da Nang province and in— I was in Intelligence and he was Infantry.' There was a pause, 'He was a Warrant Officer. He won the Military Medal. A very brave bugger and no doubt about that. He saved the lives of his entire patrol up in Phuoc Tuy and—'

Feiffer said quietly, 'Jack, I wish I didn't have to ask this, but has George Bell ever been investigated here in Hong Kong by the ICAC?'

'The anti-corruption crew? Sure. So have I. Haven't you? Hasn't everybody?'

Feiffer said, 'And?'

Ashwood was beginning to do "touchy." He was right. Feiffer knew about it. Ashwood said, 'And? *And* he was proved to be as clean as a bloody whistle! He was proved to be as clean as a bloody whistle because like a lot of hard-working honest sods those bastards get their hooks into at the urging of some dirty, second-rate rat fink little informer, he was found to be stone-cold, bloody motherless broke!' Ashwood demanded, 'What the hell are you asking me questions about George Bell for? Bloody George Bell was the bravest man I ever knew and one of those dumb buggers on his patrol he rescued in bloody Nam was me—the stupid dumbo so-called bloody Intelligence officer wandering around with a sheaf of maps and a stupid expression on his face while bloody Charlie Cong was—'

Feiffer said, 'Who was the businessman the Yakuza met at the hotel?'

Ashwood said with real vehemence, 'We've really been at our little Boy's Book Of Interrogation Methods lately, haven't we? What am I supposed to do—feel so furious about your innuendoes about my old mate Bell that I give away the secret plans to the bloody secret Zulu War muzzle loading musket without even thinking in one bloody tearful burst?' Ashwood said, 'The door to my office is open at the moment and I've got this mirage in front of my eyes that on the bloody door it says bloody *Superintendent!*' He paused to let the message sink in, 'What the hell does it say on your door?'

Feiffer said evenly, 'At the moment it says "mud." '

Ashwood drew a breath. 'The Yakuza representatives went to the Empress of India hotel to see a man called—'

'Teddy Wong?'

'—Teddy Wong. Why the hell did you ask me if you already knew? And before we play any more little tricks I'll tell you straight out that we're not sure what they saw him for. All right? Wong worked in Tokyo for a while as a hotel manager and then he was manager of a place called the Orient Dragon here in Hong Kong, in Nathan Road, and that's it. At the moment he's in insurance.' He paused for a moment, 'And that's all I know. We're in touch with the Japanese Organised Crimes Squad because if the Yakuza are involved it's something pretty big, but that's all I know!' Ashwood said warningly, 'You might try to remember that we're both on the same side.' He said with a snort, 'I've enjoyed being thumbscrewed. It relaxes me enormously, just like a good massage— *But now I've got work to do.*'

'I'm sorry about asking about Bell, Jack.'

'Yeah.' Ashwood said very seriously, 'Listen, Harry, I know that man. I was in a war with him and he saved my life.' There was a silence as he thought about something. 'We were hit by an ambush set-up upcountry and George—' He stopped and said emotionally, 'In my bloody opinion he should have got the bloody VC! He wiped out the entire ambush party while we – the rest of us – were falling about in the bloody paddy fields on our arses composing our last letters home to Mummy and wondering whether now mightn't be the time to start believing in God!' Ashwood said in a still-awed voice, 'He took that goddamned thing, Harry, and he killed the lot of them with it before you could say bloody Jack Robinson! He just picked it up and blew every last one of them away like—' He made a swallowing noise, 'What it did to those bloody Viet Cong you just wouldn't believe.' He said very seriously indeed, 'George Bell was and is the bravest man I ever knew.'

'What was "it"?'

'What do you mean?'

'What he picked up. You said he—'

Ashwood said, 'Oh, the weapon.' He asked in an irritated tone of voice, 'Do the bloody gory details really matter?'

'Maybe, yes. Isn't that why you told me the story in the first place? So I'd ask?'

There was a pause. He had said too much. Ashwood said suddenly defensively, 'So what? It was in a war—and it was all a long time ago— Right again, aren't you? Yes, it was a bloody flame-thrower! So what? It was issued to him! The bloody Australian Army issued it to him because he—' Ashwood said hopelessly, 'Damn it all, Harry, it isn't the same as bloody well going out and making one, is it?'

There was a silence.

Ashwood said desperately, *'Is it?'*

*

In the carpark ticket office, Auden said to Klaus, 'It's a false wall. It's obvious. The mugger drives his van out from behind a false wall, does the job, then, in the confusion, drives back again behind the false wall and disappears.'

Klaus flicked the switch on his console to display a picture of the left side bays on the second floor, noted there were a few empty spaces there and punched out electronic directions onto the entrance throughway panel in readiness for the next customer. Klaus said without enthusiasm, 'I suppose that's a possibility all right.'

'We've worked out why different people see the van as a different colour. It's because each side of it *is* a different colour and, depending on where they're seeing it from—' Auden said, 'It's a false wall.'

'What is?'

'Where he's hiding with his multi-coloured van. He's hiding behind a false wall somewhere and after he's mugged his victim he disappears behind it and— Doesn't that seem logical to you?'

'Sure. If you say so.'

'Well, *doesn't it?*'

Klaus said, 'Yes! Sure!' He flicked another button, more out of embarrassment than efficiency, 'It seems a lot of trouble to go to, but I suppose, yeah, sure, that's logical.' He grinned at Auden nervously, 'Um, where is this false wall? On the third floor?'

Spencer shook his head, 'Phil saw the back of the VW going down from the third floor towards the second.'

'The second then?'

Auden said, 'Ah.' He looked at Spencer, 'Come on, Bill, explain it to him the way you explained it to me.' He nudged Klaus on the arm, 'Listen to this ... '

Spencer said cautiously, thinking about it, 'Well, I'm not sure it's really right ... '

'Well then Klaus can tell you!' Auden said proudly, 'Go on, this is good. Listen to this.' He watched as Spencer took

95

out his notebook and consulted it. Auden said encouragingly, 'The first six victims were done on the second floor, right?'

Klaus said, 'Right. I think so.'

'They were. The left hand side of the second floor. And every time they saw the VW as yellow—right?' Spencer said, 'Right. And the seventh victim was mugged on the right hand side of the third floor—and he saw the van as blue.' He paused for a flash of comprehension and got none, 'Which means, that if the VW was painted different colours then the first six victims must have seen it when it was pointing one way, and the next, the seventh, when it was pointing another.' A nagging doubt crept into his mind, 'Right?' He looked down at his open notebook to make sure he had got it right.

Klaus said dubiously, 'Unless of course it was another Volkswagen.'

Auden snapped, 'Of course it wasn't another Volkswagen! How many bloody false walls and multicoloured Volkswagens do you think there are in this place?'

Klaus looked meek, 'As a matter of fact … I didn't think … there were … any?'

Auden said to Spencer, 'Go on! Go on!'

'Then the eighth victim on the third floor – in the left hand bays – he said the van was yellow again.' Spencer stopped and scratched his head thoughtfully. Spencer said cautiously, 'Um, Phil, I think that on the third floor the van should have been … um, blue … '

Auden said, 'Rubbish! You're doing fine!'

Klaus looked confused.

Spencer said gamely, 'And then, when Mr Auden here saw the same van as white – the back of it – that must have meant since he saw it going away—that on the second floor when it was yellow it must have been pointing—' Spencer said, shaking his head, 'No, it doesn't mean that at all …'

Auden said impatiently, 'It's a hiding place, see? Don't

worry about all the logic, we can get that right later. Tell him that it proves that it's a hiding place!'

Spencer, fast feeling the ashes of defeat covering him, said without confidence, 'If it was pointing one way on the third floor and then another on the second and I—' He looked at Auden with a sick expression on his face, 'Phil, I think I've got it wrong ... '

Auden took over. Auden said, 'Listen, Klaus, here's the nub. When Mr Spencer went up to the roof he looked across at the traffic lights in Canton Street and—guess what?' Auden paused dramatically, 'And—*he could see them!*'

Klaus said gently, 'Oh. Gosh. Um ... good ... ' He moved away a pace.

Auden said with triumph, '*Right!* And then when he looked out again from the third floor he *couldn't* see them because there was a building in the way!' Auden said, 'What do you think of that? All the rest of the stuff about the van pointing the wrong way towards brick walls proves it! There's not only a false wall up there on the third floor, there's an entire false floor! Why else wouldn't he be able to see the lights?' Auden said with a friendly nudge in Spencer's ribs, 'Huh? Tell me that?'

Klaus said with a nervous smile, 'I don't know. Um ... was he standing in the same position?'

'Of course he was standing in the same place! Do you think he's bloody stupid or something?' Auden turned to Spencer for an easy nod, 'Of course he was standing in the same—' He saw Spencer's face, '*You were, weren't you?*'

Spencer said, 'Um, well, um—actually, now that you mention it—' Spencer said, 'Well, actually, to tell the truth—' He looked at Klaus with admiration on his face, 'I never actually thought of that—'

'*What do you mean, you never actually thought of that?*' Auden roared, 'I've just been telling Klaus how bloody clever you are and you tell me that— *What do you mean you never thought of that?!'*

A voice from the throughway demanded in Cantonese, 'Having a good time, are you?' It was a small Chinese lady wearing glass down the front of her dress and holding the strap of what looked like a camera case in her hand. The lady, sucking in a deep breath to begin a tirade, shouted, 'Are you cops? I was upstairs on the third floor being mugged while you disgraces to your mothers were standing around here yelling at each other! I've just been mugged and robbed and I—'

Spencer said desperately, 'The Volkswagen van—did you see what colour it was?'

'Of course I saw what colour it was! I saw it when it drew up behind me and I saw it when it took off and I saw it when it made for the throughway and came down here where you cops must have just let it get away!' The lady said, 'Colour? Black! Black all over! The colour of your rotten yelling cop souls! Black! Got that? *Black!'* She demanded, 'And I want to know why you haven't caught it yet!'

Klaus gave Spencer a reassuring pat on the shoulder, thought to tell him that the basis of creative thinking was not logic, but rather blind sudden inspiration, and then, sensibly, glancing at Auden, decided against it.

Auden said to Spencer with feeling, 'So much for your bloody ideas!'

The woman reached in and began pounding on the ticket counter with her fist for action. The woman said in a fury, 'And not only wasn't it a Volkswagen van, it was a Volkswagen *car!'* She demanded, 'Well, what are you standing here for? That should be easy enough! Go find it!'

Klaus was by nature a good hearted individual and the least he thought he could do was give Spencer a nice smile.

Spencer gazed at him and because by nature he was also a good hearted individual, tried to smile back.

*

The missing fourth floor in the carpark had been measured out, looked at from every possible angle, listened for with taps on the ceilings and foot stamps on the roof, sounded with shouts, yells and number countings, the generator room had been searched, the traffic lights angle rechecked, and, finally, one thing about the missing fourth floor had become painfully crystal clear.

There was no missing fourth floor.

Halfway down the third floor bays, Spencer paused. He turned back to Auden. 'If the van is blue, white and yellow and it points in the wrong direction and—'

Auden said, 'Shut up.'

'—and doesn't go through false walls or up into secret fourth floors because there aren't any secret fourth floors, then—'

'I don't want to hear it!'

'—and if it turns into a black sedan ... '

Auden said, 'Not another word!'

'—and if you say you saw it on the TV screen going down and it didn't pass us—'

Auden said menacingly, 'I'm warning you, Spencer ... '

'Then the prime thing to realise is that—'

Auden said, 'Is that the van or the car or whatever the hell it is—'

Spencer said expectantly, 'Yes? Yes?'

'—*then it doesn't bloody well exist, does it?*'

Spencer said, 'AH-HA!' Spencer said, *'Right!'*

'Oh, God!' Auden said at the end of his patience, 'What the hell do you mean right? I heard the glass smash and then I heard the—' Auden said suddenly, 'No, I didn't.' Auden furrowed his brow, 'If I heard the glass smash, why the hell didn't I hear the Volkswagen's engine rev up when it took off to get away?' He looked at Spencer, 'I didn't hear an engine at all.'

'And neither did I on the roof!' Spencer said with a glint in his eye, 'We didn't hear it because—' He turned to face Auden with a sudden grin of comprehension on his face, 'Time in the little grey cells of the brain—'

Auden said, 'Sherlock Holmes?'

'Hercule Poirot.' Spencer said, 'We didn't hear it because—' He reached in suddenly under his coat and drew out his revolver, 'You're right! You've seen through it! We didn't hear it because—*because it doesn't exist!*'

'But I saw it! I—' Auden, being led yet again, said suddenly, 'Oh no you don't! This time you tell me what the hell you're drivelling about!'

Spencer's gleam lit up even further into a positive beam. 'I'm drivelling about—' He snapped open the cylinder of his gun and took out a single round nosed lead bullet, '—about the little man who—' He quoted happily,

'As I was going up the stair,
I saw a little man who wasn't there,
He wasn't there again today,
I wish, I wish he'd go away.'

He went forward with the bullet in his hand like a pencil and scored a deep cross on one of the pylons leading to the throughway and then another on the floor of the through-way itself, 'I'm drivelling about—' He caught sight of a little Fiat Bambino car parked in the centre space of one of the bays and, looking inside it, said, 'Ah-ha! Of course, just in the right spot!' He ordered Auden, 'See the side window of that Fiat? I want you to smash it!'

'Aye? Who does it belong to?'

Spencer said, glancing quickly into the back window of the vehicle, 'Ah-ha! The mugger!'

'The mugger owns a Volkswagen!'

Spencer said, 'Ah-ha-ha—*ha!*'

'If that's the mugger's car, then you know who the mugger is!' Auden, being sucked in yet again, demanded, 'In that case, why don't we just arrest him?'

'Because we can't.'

'Why not?'

Spencer said happily, 'Ah, ha-ha, ha! We can't arrest him because, obviously—'

Auden said, 'What? What?' The back seat of the car was piled with magazines and periodicals in some sort of foreign language. Auden said, 'What? What?'

The Fiat looked brand new, pristine, much loved, possibly even, if he was right, paid for up to the last hire purchase usurer's decimal interest point. Spencer looking at it and grinning said easily, 'Obviously, Phil, because —because *there isn't any mugger!*'

There was a car coming up the throughway from the ticket office and he listened to the roar of its engine as the driver changed down for the gradient and looked happy.

*

In the Detectives' Room Feiffer had two names printed on his blotter, both surrounded by doodled squares and question marks.

Anthony Lam?

Teddy Wong?

Looking at the phone, he wrote another name on the list and put a question mark next to that as well.

Chief Fire Safety Officer George Bell?

It was 3.45 p.m. and The Spaceman's next move was less than eight minutes away from completion.

In the cells The Green Slime looked at his watch and began sobbing again.

11

In Room 517 of the Empress of India hotel, Hideki Shimada San, sipping at his Scotch and water, said definitely, 'No, it is an inescapable fact that we have to have at least a couple of thousand people slaughtered at one go.' A middle aged Japanese dressed in a thousand islands Hawaiian shirt, Shimada said, 'You just can't find anyone to kill. In Tokyo these days, as soon as you find a suitable spot and get together the victims the cops are in demanding to see your traffic clearance and your explosives licence and then, if you want to bring in a few heavy weapons for the Japanese Army to defeat the monster with, you get the Japanese Army along saying that they're now called the Japanese Defence Force and under the terms of international agreements they're not allowed to have heavy weapons.' He sighed, 'And then after you've modified them the Red Army decides to steal the heavy weapons, and then you get the cops again—'

K.S. Mukherjee sitting opposite him in an easy chair said, 'In India we have the same trouble. Mrs Gandhi, now she's back in power again and beaten all the court cases, thinks if anyone is going to be seen on film triumphing over evil, it ought to be her.' He asked, 'This film you want to co-produce, does it have any city flattening in it?'

'Yokohama, Mysore and Delhi.'

Mukherjee said, 'Fine! Disembowelling?'

102

To a Japanese that was a bit of a sensitive issue. Shimada said, 'Hmm. We can put some in if you want it.'

'Well, we do really if we want to pull the Sikh section of the audience.'

'O.K.' To get a little you had to give a little. Shimada said, 'This monster we propose, it's sort of like a cannibal. Is there any sort of beast it shouldn't touch for India?'

'We wouldn't be too keen on cows.'

Shimada said, 'Right.'

'Or pigs for that matter.'

'O.K.'

Mukherjee said quickly, 'But there's no objection to people of course.'

'Right.'

Mukherjee asked, 'What about you? If we do this film, obviously we'll want to do a little re-writing. Anything the Japanese audience might find offensive?'

Shimada considered the tastes of the Japanese audience for a while, 'No, nothing.'

'Great.' Mukherjee sipped at his drink and thought he had a deal going here. 'O.K., we can get all that by the Indian censor provided we blow up Calcutta rather than Delhi. Does that suit you?'

Shimada looked curious.

'The censor's from Delhi.' Mukherjee said, 'Right, now I've got your word on it there's at least one good disembowelling, a fair bit of cannibalism, lots of peasant slaughter and gunfire, and that the heroes – an Indian insect-expert and a Japanese underwater specialist – defeat the monster in equal measure, right?'

Shimada said, 'Right.'

Mukherjee said, 'As long as there's no kissing. The Indian censors just won't wear kissing.'

Shimada said, 'Oh.' He thought of the porno trade in Tokyo, 'The Japanese classical tradition has a long history of—'

Mukherjee, not one to put obstacles in the way where they could be avoided, said, 'For the tit trade we can do a dirty version of film using stand-ins. We can shoot that part here in Hong Kong.'

Shimada made a grave nod.

Mukherjee, the deal concluded, said with regret, 'I'm sorry Mukherjee-Gopol-Mukherjee hasn't got a film to show here at the premieres—but we've had a little trouble recently with one of our studio actresses suing us over something we said about her sex life in the papers.   He looked around, 'Where are you keeping THE IONO-SPHERE CRUMBLES?'

Shimada said, 'MELTS.' He nodded in the direction of his bed, 'Under the bed. I'd have it in a distributor's safe if this was Tokyo, but until the premieres get seen by the distributors here I haven't got a distributor.' He dropped his voice, 'From what I heard, half the distributors in Hong Kong are paying out protection to the Triads and if I left it there with one of them it'd be out on the streets in pirate cassettes before you could say—' was going to say 'Banzai', but decided against it, 'Before you could say Indian-Japanese Co-Production.' There was a knock at the door and Shimada said, 'That's probably them now come to tell me that the Second World War isn't over and Japanese film screening rights come under the heading of post-war reparations.'

The knocking came again. Mukherjee said, 'More likely it's this fucking Spaceman character come to sell us the film rights to his life story.' He asked, 'Do you want me to answer it?'

'Thanks.' Shimada went to freshen his drink. 'If it's the hotel manager tell him I'd like a few coolies sent up here with sledge hammers to break up the rocks in my mattress.' He poured himself a measure of Scotch and whooshed soda into it from a siphon. 'If it's one of my ex-wives—' He glanced anxiously at Mukherjee as he crossed the room and thought about Indian morality, 'Tell them they're impostors and I don't have any ex-wives.' He heard the door open. The soda siphon was almost empty. He said suddenly irritably, turning, 'Well, who the hell is it?'

It was The Spaceman. He had his petrol gun in his hand.

The Spaceman stood a little outside the open door gazing at them through his black opaque Perspex faceplate, the weapon in his hand steady and unmoving.

The Spaceman shook his head and raised his free gloved hand to his helmet to silence them.

The gun moved higher. There was a clicking sound. Shimada dropped his soda siphon.

Mukherjee and Shimada, their tongues sticking to the roofs of their mouths, froze instantly in terror.

*

In the ticket office, Spencer said earnestly to Klaus, 'I think I've got it. I think that all the victims of the mugger got it wrong and that the Volkswagen kombi van wasn't yellow at all.' He looked down at the console controlling the television cameras and gave it a stroke, 'I've been trying to look at this logically, like a computer, and I've come to the conclusion that unless the Volkswagen doesn't exist—that it has to be white.' He smiled at Klaus expectantly.

Klaus said, interested, 'Oh?'

'Yes, I've put all the information through my mind like a computer and I've realised that one of the important factors I'd missed was that in each of the nine muggings the victim was just an ordinary person suddenly put under great stress and that therefore they might have made a mistake. I've then run through all the other bits of data at my disposal and come up with the fact that the one trained, reliable observer who saw the vehicle – not under stress but calmly and clearly here on the TV screen (Mr Auden) – saw it as white.' He paused, looking anxious, 'So therefore I've come to the conclusion that the vehicle involved is a white Volkswagen kombi van and that everyone else made a mistake about it.' He glanced up in the direction of the ceiling, 'Mr Auden's on the second floor because that's where he thinks the mugger will strike next and all we need now is one good sighting and it'll be certain.' Spencer said with a tinge of disappointment in his voice, 'Sherlock Holmes wouldn't have fought the coming of the machine, he would have welcomed it.'

Klaus said, 'I always thought myself that Holmes was really a bit of a nut on science rather than deduction.'

'You're right of course.' Spencer said, 'We all imagine the world the way we'd like it to be, but really, logically, data-wise there's only one truth in it and that's the truth the machines tell us, isn't it?'

Klaus said happily, 'Yeah, that's right!'

Spencer grinned at him, 'The only alternative to the inescapable conclusion that the vehicle is a white VW kombi is that—that it doesn't exist at all.' He made a chuckling noise, 'And then I'd be back to square one and the false wall and floor theory.'

Klaus said, 'I think you've covered that one pretty fully already. If there was a false wall here I'd know about it.' He indicated a smaller console on the desk, 'That's a car counter. It counts how many cars go in and how many go out. If there was a false floor it'd show that not enough cars were parked in here when I pressed the CARPARK FULL button and the owners would be down on me like a ton of bricks.' He said with a grin, 'If I find a carpark in Australia that doesn't have one of those counters maybe I'll brick up a floor, rent it out for a million dollars a year and claim the carpark's full when it isn't.' He said with a smile, 'No, you can't beat the machine, not really.'

Spencer nodded.

Klaus asked, 'Where did you say Mr Auden was?'

'On the second floor.'

Klaus said, 'To be honest, Mr Spencer, I had the impression that it was Mr Auden rather than you who liked machines.'

Spencer said, 'I'm not so set in my ways I can't see the shape of the future when it's presented to me full-on.' A line of cars came through the barrier and went upwards at the direction of the electronic arrow and floor number board towards the second floor. Spencer said, 'Mr Auden can keep an eye on them when they park.' He glanced at his watch and seemed to be counting something. 'It's really well laid out this carpark—it only takes about thirty seconds to get from the entrance to the top floor.'

Klaus said with an easy grin, 'The false floor theory again?'

Embarrassed, Spencer said, 'Yes.' He grinned sheepishly, 'I'm afraid when I get an idea in my head—'

Klaus said, 'The lay out of the carpark was designed by a computer. That's why it's so efficient.'

Spencer said sadly, 'Yeah ...' He brightened up, 'All I need is one white Volkswagen kombi van ...'

'And what if you don't get it?' Klaus said reasonably, 'There aren't any false walls or floors in the place however hard you look—'

Spencer said with conviction, 'Then I'm going to spend the rest of my life working out just how it's done! It wouldn't have beaten Holmes for five minutes so it shouldn't beat me for more than five weeks.' Spencer said with rising anger, 'If I have to I'll grill every one of the victims so hard their eyes will drop out. If I have to—'

Klaus said, 'But you've already said they're not reliable. That they said the van was yellow and blue and black and whatever because—'

Spencer said, 'If I have to I'll have them relive the experience under hypnosis – under truth drugs—'

'But it's white. You said Mr Auden was the only reliable witness—'

'No one else has seen it as white except him!'

Klaus said, 'I did! I saw it for a second on the screen when Mr Auden saw it and I saw it as white too.'

'I don't know.' Spencer pursed his lips, 'I just don't know ...'

Klaus said, 'What if you saw it yourself?'

'Ah, then I'd be sure it's white. Then I'd be sure the witnesses didn't know what they were talking about.' Spencer said grittily, 'Then I'd know that there really was a Volkswagen and that it was white and that somehow, it got past us.' He paused for a moment, 'I'd know there wasn't a false floor or a wall in here where it changed colour and hid.'

Klaus considered it for a moment. He shrugged, thinking. He said, 'Hmm, maybe there is a false wall—' He glanced down at the console on his desk, 'If there isn't, I get the impression you'll have all the victims in this goddamned place giving statements to the cops for the next twenty years.'

Spencer said firmly, 'Twenty five.' He glanced at his watch.

Klaus said, 'Hmm ...' There was a sudden terrible sound of glass breaking from somewhere up on the second or third floor and Klaus gasped out, 'My God, another one!'

Spencer rushed to the console and began pressing buttons. The picture on the television screen exploded into lines and snow and Klaus pushed past him and got up the picture of the ground floor right. Spencer said, 'No, it was high up! Quick, punch up the third floor—quick!'

'But Mr Auden's on the *second* floor!'

'Quick, before Mr Auden gets up to the third. This time we'll see it ourselves!' Spencer said, 'Come on, damn it, do you want to be around here for the next twenty five years?'

Find me that white Volkswagen on the third floor—quick!'

Klaus pressed a button and there it was. Klaus said, 'There! Look! It's going away towards the throughway! Mr Auden isn't there yet. It is white! Look!' Klaus wrenched open the ticket office door, 'Quick, after it!'

Spencer turned around from the console with an evil smile on his face. He thought about it for a moment, shrugged, and then said lazily, 'No, let's wait until it comes down here.' He saw Klaus start to come forward and leaned over the console, 'Let me save you the trouble of pushing up the other floors.' He flicked a few buttons. 'Or even the other third floor bays.' Another button—

Spencer said in mock surprise, 'Oh my goodness, the white Volkswagen seems to have disappeared.' He leaned forward and put his finger on the screen, 'And now, wonder of wonders, I can see where I put the crosses on the pylons not ten minutes ago.' He turned to fix Klaus with a steely eye, 'The crosses must be able to do the same disappearing trick as the white Volkswagen because a moment ago when I saw the Volkswagen fleeing, the crosses *weren't bloodywell there!*' The picture on the screen showed Auden standing at the smashed side window of the Fiat, his Colt Python in his hand, gazing at the line of crosses going away from him on the pylons. Spencer said, 'And my goodness me, Mr Auden seems to have learned the trick too – because he was standing on the third floor all the time – *he was the one who smashed the Fiat's window!*' Spencer reached in under his coat, withdrew his handcuffs, and laid them on top of the console significantly and said in a voice that brooked no discussion, 'Come over to this console and show me where the video tape button is.' He saw Klaus about to protest, 'The video tape button that cuts in a reel of film showing a white Volkswagen disappearing into nothingness on the third floor!' He demanded, 'There never was any mugger or any Volkswagen, was there? The victims smashed their own car windows and—what? Hid the valuables that were supposed to be stolen in their car boots?'

Klaus sighed a long sigh. 'Under the rear seats.'

'What the hell did they say the thing was yellow for? And blue? And black? And—when all the time you had this film set up to prove the bloody thing was white?'

'The stupid bastards didn't understand English properly! The first one thought I said it was a yellow van and then next—' Klaus said with rising disgust for the human race, 'The stupid thing about people as opposed to machines is that they all think they're so goddamned clever and they just don't realise just how—'

Spencer said maliciously, 'Yeah!'

'—how—' Klaus' voice trailed off, 'Just how stupid they really are ...'

Spencer put on his official policeman's voice, 'You can remember that when you get out on bail before your hearing and you have to pay to have your car window repaired.' He nodded to himself. It was only poetic justice. Spencer said, 'Machines are all right in their place, but when it comes to working something out—'

Klaus said, 'What car window repaired?'

'The Fiat Bambino on the third floor. It was your car. It struck me as only right and proper that if someone's car window was going to get smashed to prove how it was done then it was only fair that it should be yours.' Spencer said avuncularly, 'It's all been a valuable lesson to you—seeing the superiority of a human brain when it comes to working something out. And if you want my opinion I just don't think it's a good thing to let children have pocket calculators and things like that at school in the first place. It stunts the brain. I *worked out* that it was your car because (a) it had German licence plates and (b) because the back was full of computer and electronics magazines and (c)—'

Klaus said, 'I don't own a car.'

Spencer said, 'You're under arrest. I have to warn you that anything you may say—'

'I tell you, I don't own a goddamned car! I can't even drive!'

Spencer said, 'Rubbish.' He saw Auden coming towards the ticket office looking pleased with himself and called out, 'Phil, that was his car, wasn't it?'

'Sure. You looked it up. You said so.'

'No, I deduced it because of the—'

Klaus, his misery complete, shouted, 'Don't you try to stick a car stealing rap on me too! All I've done is a little fraud so don't you try and fit me up as some sort of hardened—'

Auden said, 'What do you mean you *deduced* it? You rang Central Computer from outside and got a make on it and you—' His eyes widened, 'Didn't you?' He saw Spencer look away. He said, aghast, 'You saw the Fiat had German licence plates on it and—'

Spencer said quickly, 'Well, no, actually it had Hong Kong licence plates, but it had a ... a national sticker on the back.' He grinned nervously. 'It had CD on it. That stands for Something ... *Deutschland.*' He saw Auden's face, 'Doesn't it?'

Something ... Deutschland ...

True to form, even at the moment of his triumph, Spencer of Baker Street considered all the other ... Spencer said urgently, 'Yes! Something ... *Deutschland* ...!'

Or ...

... or ...

Spencer said in a strangled voice, 'Or, or—'

Diplomatic ... Corps ...?

Auden, hopping about in red faced fury, the evidence of broken glass and scratched revolver barrel all over his person, shouted, 'You didn't check with Central Computer? You just—' Auden shouted at the top of his voice, 'Jesus Christ in Heaven, Spencer, what the hell do you think bloody machines are *for?*'

*

Glancing up through the open door of the Detectives' Room, O'Yee said aghast, 'It's him! He's got out again!'

Feiffer said, 'Who?'

'Him! Goddamned Houdini! *The Green Slime!*' The Green Slime was on the phone in the empty charge room, saying in Chinese, 'Are you sure? Are you certain?' O'Yee shouted, 'You! Hey, you!' He knocked over a sheaf of papers in his haste to get out from behind his desk, *'You!'* He shouted to Feiffer as he took off out of the door, 'By God, I know who's going to arrest him this time—*I am!*' The Slime's hand on the telephone receiver was trembling with fear. The Slime said over and over in Cantonese, 'Are you certain? Are you sure?'

O'Yee said, 'Got you!' He grabbed The Slime by the finned collar and wrenched him about, 'By God, this time you're going to tell me—' O'Yee tore the phone from the man's grasp and jammed it against his ear, 'Who is this? Speak up! *Who is this?*'

The line went dead.

O'Yee had The Slime in a stranglehold around the neck. Twisting the man's repulsive masked face to him, he demanded, 'You! Who arrested you? By God, if you don't—'

The Slime, gasping, said, 'Special Constable Jensen Ho!'

O'Yee saw Feiffer at the door to the Detectives' Room and decided not to strangle The Slime in front of witnesses. O'Yee shrieked, 'I don't even know what the hell you were in the cell for in the first place!'

'For nothing!' The Slime broke loose and stood back, panting, ready to duck O'Yee's clenching hands, 'I was in there for nothing! I'm trying to tell you who arrested me and you won't even listen!' The Slime, at the end of his control, shouted, 'Special Constable Jensen Ho—that's who arrested me!' He saw O'Yee make a move towards him and yelled to halt him, 'That's why I was arrested in the first place! Special Constable Jensen Ho—'

O'Yee said, *Who the hell's Special Constable Jensen Ho?*

The Slime, hesitating a moment and then glancing at the mute telephone, drew a breath.

The Green Slime said quietly, 'I am. I'm Special Constable Jensen Ho.'

He seemed a little disappointed, with all the hints he had given him, that the man had not realised it from the beginning.

*

In the foyer of the hotel, the pained look on Constable Lee's face was increasing in intensity. Standing with his knees pressed hard together and his hands clutched together on his belt buckle, Constable Lee said graphically, 'Ohh—ah—yah ...' He looked at Constable Sun.

Sun said, 'Aii—!' He grimaced at Lee, his face in pain, and said between clenched teeth, 'You ... too?'

Lee said, 'Mmmm—ah.' A little to one side of the million dollars there was a corridor with an arrow and a painted representation of the male of the species on the wall. Lee said, 'If I don't go in a minute, I'll burst!'

Sun said, nodding, 'Mmm—yaa ...' He was going red in the face.

Lee looked suddenly heavenwards. 'It's no good, I have to go! If anyone wants to steal the million dollars then they can steal it.' Lee said, looking desperate, 'I have to go!' He turned and made off quickly for the sign.

Sun, his straining bladder muscles rooting him to the spot, said in an urgent whisper, 'For heaven's sake, hurry!' Across the foyer, in the bar, there was a barman washing glasses. The sound of running water almost unhinged his reason. He called out in a prayer as Lee hurried away down the magic corridor towards pure, blessed relief, 'Hurry! In heaven's name—*hurry!*'

*

Under The Spaceman's gun, Shimada and Mukherjee were pressed against the fifth floor corridor wall edging their way towards the open door to the stairs. The Spaceman's gun followed them, the black faceplate on The Spaceman's helmet reflecting them opaquely.

Shimada said to The Spaceman, 'We're not who you think we are ... we're nobodies ... we're ... ' He hit a little side table and almost knocked it down. He made a grab for the overbalancing lamp on top of it. Shimada said, 'It's just a—! It's just a ... lamp ... !'

Mukherjee bumped into him against the wall and gave him a nudge he hoped The Spaceman didn't notice. Mukherjee said, 'For God's sake, don't talk! Just ...' Shimada seemed to have stopped by the side table. Mukherjee gasped at him, 'Go on, go on—!'

The Spaceman heard a sound and jerked his head quickly in the direction of the service elevator at the far end of the corridor.

Shimada said soothingly, 'There's nothing! It's just—' The Spaceman's gun came back to him, 'It's all right! It's just—' He hit something with his shoe – an electric socket – and pressed his hands flatter against the wall and edged past it like a child expecting to be hit by an unpredictable father, 'It's nothing—just a—' He saw the open door to the stairs, 'Honest, we'll do exactly what we're—' He thought The Spaceman might not know about the stairs. He halted, wondering if he could sacrifice Mukherjee and make a run for it.

Mukherjee jabbed him in the ribs with his elbow. 'Move! Move!'

114

Shimada felt glued to the wall by the palms of his hands. The stairs were less than ten feet away. Shimada felt his mouth open and shut, but no sound came out. Shimada, hiccoughing with fear, got out, 'Can we ... go down the stairs ...?'

The Spaceman, immobile, listening, nodded his head.

Shimada said, 'Thank you, thank you ...' He made a series of happy hee-hee sounds and nodded happily at Mukherjee. He said urgently to The Spaceman, bowing, 'Thank you, oh thank—'

The muzzle of the flame gun seemed to be dripping a fine fluid. Mukherjee grated out from somewhere deep in his dry throat, *'Get on with it, you stupid Japanese bastard!'* The stairs were less than five feet away from Shimada's right hand. Mukherjee said in a series of breathless grunts, 'Move, move, *move!'*

Shimada's hand touched the door jamb to the stairs. He halted. The Spaceman's gun followed him and then halted too, pointing at his chest. Shimada said, 'Wife and ...' He hiccoughed, 'We're just very small fish, we're—' He moved on a single shuffling pace and stood with his back to the open door to freedom, 'Can we—?'

The Spaceman lifted up his gun a fraction. He seemed to be thinking.

Mukherjee said carefully, 'May we—um ...?'

The gun pointed squarely at Shimada's chest and then moved to bring itself to bear on Mukherjee. The gun made a clicking sound.

The Spaceman nodded.

The message was clear: die, or run like hell.

Shimada and Mukherjee almost colliding with each other at the top of the stairs, ran like hell.

*

In the Detectives' Room, The Green Slime said urgently,

'My wife and children—the Triads. I—' He brushed at his forehead and took the rubber Slime mask from his cheeks and forehead, 'They, I—' He drew a breath, 'I'm Special Constable Jensen Ho and I put myself in the cell so I could be blameless, so he wouldn't—' He stared at O'Yee with something approaching hatred, 'But you were too stupid to work out who I was!'

'I *still* don't know who you are!'

'I'm Jensen Ho!'

'Who the hell is Jensen Ho?'

'The Special Constable who—'

Feiffer said slowly, '—who works for the Hong Kong Safe And Strongbox Company.'

'Yes!' The Slime turned to O'Yee, 'Why couldn't *you* have worked that out? I'm the man the police call in when there's a safe they have to get open or when there's a lock that—' He opened his hands in mute appeal to all that was reasonable in the world, 'Who else in the Colony do you think could open a cell with nothing but a nail or a match and a piece of string? *I'm Special Constable Jensen Ho!*'

Feiffer said, 'What were you doing in the cells?'

'I was hiding. I was protecting myself from—' The Slime wiped sweat from his face with his hand, 'I thought he'd think I'd been arrested on the way. I got a phone call from him saying that unless I co-operated the Triads would kill my family. That's why I got into one of the cells—so he'd think I'd wanted to do the job but I'd just had bad luck on the way and been arrested.' He turned to O'Yee, 'That's why I shouted and yelled and escaped—so you'd beat me up and make it look good. *And you didn't!* You were so busy doing whatever else you were doing you didn't even stop to think. I wanted you to guess who I was—*but you didn't!*' The Slime said, 'It's the forty five million dollars! The lock on the case holding the forty five million dollars!'

Feiffer looked at him.

'The one on the case in the Empress of India hotel!' The

Slime, a helpless victim to the assembled stupidity of the world, said, 'Where else?'

'What forty five million dollars in a case at the hotel? There's *one* million in a—'

'He said that it involved forty five million American dollars and he was from the Triads and that, for that sort of money, if I didn't open the lock for him while he created a diversion, the lives of my family wouldn't be worth a—'

Feiffer said, 'Who?'

The Slime, his eyes filling with tears, said desperately, '*Him!* The Triad man! He said he'd be dressed up as a—he said he'd—' The Slime, staring at O'Yee said, 'What else could I do? I couldn't think of any other way of getting out of it and protecting my family at the same time. I just—' All of a sudden, like a balloon abruptly deflated, he sank into a chair and seemed to shrink. Tears flowed down his cheeks. 'He said he'd meet me in the carpark by the flying saucer.'

The Green Slime – Special Constable Jensen Ho – said, 'The Spaceman. Teddy Wong. He said if I didn't help, he'd kill my family.' He asked, 'What else could I have done?'

*

It was no good. He couldn't last another moment. Clenching his teeth, Constable Sun made for the toilets hoping to meet Constable Lee on his way out.

He glanced back at the million dollars for a moment. It all seemed quiet. He saw the door marked MEN in Chinese and English and pushed it gratefully open.

A voice shrieked out in English in pure terror, 'Oh, NO!' and Sun turned back again to see an Indian and a squat Japanese transfixed to the end of the corridor in horror staring out into the foyer in the direction of the service elevator.

More goddamned lunatics and vampires and publicity stunts. Sun went into the men's room and slammed the door.

People were running. The Spaceman's gun was trained squarely on the case containing the million dollars and the flock of million dollar watchers made for parts unknown. The five flights of stairs down which they had just run beckoned to Shimada and Mukherjee and they turned at full speed and began running up them again.

There was the faintest fine clear liquid dripping from the nozzle of The Spaceman's flame gun.

He waited until everyone was clear, pulled the trigger and, setting off the petrol cascading around the money case like a wind, reduced the million dollars inside it to ash.

The corridor was in a direct line with the money. The concussion of the petrol exploding blew the men's room door completely off its hinges and, smashing into the long room-length mirror inside, narrowly missed Constable Lee brushing his hair and scattered shards of glass and wood all over the scrubbed-down spotless white tiles on the floor.

12

The diver's knife had come from a wall display in the Lagoon Bar of the hotel. A heavy, double edged weapon with a thick steel haft, it made a clanging sound as Teddy Wong drew it from its brass scabbard and held it ready. The rest of Room 511 was empty: he paused outside the bathroom door with the knife held ready in his hand and tried the door knob, then, before it turned, changed his mind and got down on his knees to look through the crack under the door. It was dark. If he was waiting inside there for him, then he had the light off. Wong thought for a moment. The light could only be turned on and off from outside. He got up again and looked at the switch. Off. If he was waiting there inside for him then he had gone in with the light off and was there in the darkness.

Wong ran through a mental picture of the hotel bathrooms—they were standard: a sink on the left, toilet facing the door, tiles on the floor, and the shower and bath recess on the right, hidden by a plastic curtain. Wong touched at the point of the knife and put his head against the door to listen.

There was the faintest sound of water dripping.

He put his hand on the door knob again and gave it the slightest turn before it engaged the levers and made a creaking sound.

Wong ran his tongue across his lips and put a little more pressure on the knob and stopped the creaking sound. The dripping water as the door came open echoed in the tiled, windowless room.

Wong flipped the light on and, with his eyes hard and glittering, stared at the closed shower curtain and listened for breathing.

The hot water tap in the sink on his left went steadily drip, drip, drip into the porcelain basin.

Wong grasped the knife hard in his hand, and, tensing himself, went forward and took hold of the plastic curtain.

His heart was thumping like a triphammer.

He wrenched the curtain aside.

Nothing.

The room The Spaceman was using as his temporary staging post had to be Room 512, next door.

Teddy Wong's mouth was trembling with fear. He felt a wave of nausea rise up from his stomach and, still gripping the knife, he retched into the toilet bowl convulsively.

*

On the phone in the hotel foyer, the Commander's voice came as an order, 'Harry, you're going to have to evacuate the hotel and that's all there is to it.'

The stench of smouldering carpet and melted glass and plastic was still almost overwhelming in the foyer. Feiffer coughed back a lungful of thick, oily black smoke and demanded, 'To where? Where am I supposed to evacuate it to? I've just had to fight my way in past the front desk through a throng of guests who don't have to be evacuated—they'll go entirely of their own free will. But the fact of the matter is *that with the Congress there's just nowhere to put them!*'

'Then we'll get the Army to take them in.'

'What Army? This isn't the nineteenth century, Neil, with entire brigades of Cavalry chaps based in the Empire, this is the good old Socialist cutback eighties. I doubt whether the Army at its current strength in Hong Kong could take in a stray cat from the street, let alone upwards of almost twelve hundred people from a six hundred room hotel.' He saw Superintendent Ashwood pause in the foyer for a moment to discuss something with Deputy Chief Fire Safety Officer Chang, 'It looks like now we may be starting to get a few solid leads—'

The Commander said, 'Leads like what? Like that some rubber-suited lunatic calling himself The Green Slime tells you that an insurance man named Teddy Wong wants him to open a glass case containing forty five million dollars – which doesn't exist – so that selfsame Wong can blow it up with a petrol gun? Or that—'

Feiffer was silent.

'—or that The Spaceman leaves Triad calling cards in elevators and the Triad Bureau tell you that's the last thing the Triads would do? Or that another maniac gets messages on smoke and water telling him that—'

Feiffer said, 'That was Wong's work. I've spoken to Lam again about the messages and it looks like every time he got one, for one reason or another, Wong had been in his office a few minutes earlier. Because Wong was supposed to be his friend he didn't—'

'But according to Wong the Singapore backers are the villains. And according to every other reliable source in the world they're not!' The Commander said, 'I hate to state the obvious, but if the million dollars is insured by Wong where's the profit in his burning it or stealing it?'

'I don't know.'

'I know you don't know. The Spaceman – or whatever he calls himself in his lunatic bloody fantasies, has got one thing in mind and one thing only – and that's to set fire to the whole Hong Bay bloody street map which I, for one, don't intend to let happen!'

Feiffer said firmly, 'Neil, he didn't burn two producers

on the fifth floor, he came all the way down to the foyer for the money. If he was just some sort of psycho—'

'He *is* some sort of psycho! That's the way a psycho acts—without rational explanation—'

'There are no sprinklers on the fifth floor because the carpets and curtains up there aren't nylon, they're—'

'So what?'

'So, if he wanted to burn the place down and/or aimlessly slaughter the happy multitudes, why the hell didn't he do it then? If he'd let fly on the fifth or the sixth floor the place would have gone up like a Roman Candle. The fact that he seems to have limited himself to act only on the floors where there are reliable automatic systems suggests that—'

'Yes?'

'Well, that he's not going to burn the hotel down anyway!'

'Then what *is* he going to do?'

'I don't know!' He saw Ashwood look over at him and dropped his voice, 'Look, Wong was with Lam when the money went up. According to Lam, Wong was – to put it mildly – astounded. I think if Wong's involved there's some sort of double-cross going on—'

'From who?'

'I don't know. I'm not sure. I think all this stuff about Triads and million dollars and the Japanese Yakuza may be just some sort of—' He was going to say "smokescreen" —'I think there may be someone behind it who—' It was no good. Feiffer said directly, 'The only person in the Colony so far as I can see who has access to a firefighting suit of the right type is Chief Fire Safety Officer George Bell.'

There was a moment of stunned silence and then the Commander said evenly, 'What did you say?'

'He's supposed to be at the Roxy movie house seeing a movie called *The Towering Inferno*—'

The Commander said coldly, 'Then, knowing Bell, that's exactly where he undoubtedly is.'

'But the only trouble is that the manager of the Roxy tells me by phone that they don't happen to be showing *The Towering Inferno* at the moment!' He said quickly before the Commander could react, 'And neither is anyone else in the whole of bloody South East Asia! They're all showing sci fi and horror movies. *The Towering Inferno* is a disaster movie.' Feiffer put the knife in, 'And George Bell's car, far from being parked anywhere near a movie theatre, is parked outside this bloody hotel in the street!'

'Are you trying to tell me George Bell is The Spaceman?' The Commander said furiously, 'I've known Bell for years!'

'Everyone has known Bell for years!' Feiffer saw Ashwood glance over trying to hear, 'I'm just telling you what seems to be coming to the fore. One of my Constables told me that Bell was seen in the foyer before the fire and he was—'

'Then he was just—'

Feiffer said desperately, 'Neil, the reason we haven't searched this hotel from top to bottom is that a firefighting suit of the type The Spaceman uses will fit into something no larger than a small box. In fact, Bell's own personal suit, according to Chang, is carried in the back of his car in a briefcase. I'm having that looked into now.' He paused for a moment, 'And Bell, when he came in here—'

'Find bloody Wong!'

'I'm trying to!'

'Then ask bloody Wong about Bell!' The Commander said warningly, 'By God, Harry, if that man's accused of something he didn't do— That man ...'

Feiffer finished for him, 'Yeah, he was the bravest man you ever knew.'

There was a pause, then the Commander said quietly, 'Yes, he was. A niece of mine set fire to her parents' apartment over on Leighton Hill with a box of matches she'd found in a drawer—and the local Brigade people wouldn't go into the building because of the fumes, and if it hadn't been for George Bell—' He gave an order, 'You find bloody Wong and even if you have to beat it out of him I want to know that Bell has got nothing to do with all this!' He paused for a moment, not to be sidetracked, 'And if you haven't come to some sort of conclusion in the next few hours, like it or not, theories or not—I'm having the entire bloody hotel and everything around it evacuated faster than you can say fucking *S. S. Titanic!*'

'I'm not sure that isn't exactly what he wants us to do!'

'What he wants us to do! What counts is what I want us to do!' The Commander said with uncharacteristic tyranny, 'And that, Feiffer, so far as you are concerned, is the authentic voice of God! And I don't care if you have to kick down every one of the six hundred rooms in that bloody place—'

Feiffer said abruptly, 'Five hundred and ninety eight ...'

'—you just do it! You find Wong! Find him and get the bloody truth out of him—and, above all, you get bloody George Bell right out of your bloody mind! Do you hear me?'

The remains of the million dollars were sinking in a swamp of sprinkler fluid and foam. Feiffer saw Ashwood looking down at it.

Auden and Spencer were outside with Bell's car. Feiffer said to the Commander quietly, 'Yes, sir,' put the phone down gently, and went over to Ashwood to distract him for a few moments.

*

In the street, Auden said, 'You can read, right?' He extended a rigid finger in the direction of the licence plate of the green Range Rover parked near the entrance to the hotel's front carpark, 'That's the licence number you've got written down on your little scrap of paper, right?'

Spencer said for the third time, 'Yes! Do you want to see it?'

'No, I don't want to see it! I might be bloody colour blind or something! That's the plate, right?'

'Right!'

Auden walked around to the side of the vehicle. There was a decal on it with the colophon of the Hong Kong Fire Service and a little additional legend reading, *Chief Fire Safety Officer, Hong Bay—Official.* Auden said, 'Right? No CDs or bloody DCs or—that's the badge, right?'

Spencer said, *'Right!'*

Auden drew a breath, 'All right.' He drew his long barreled Colt Python from his holster, glanced around to make sure the coast was clear, and said pessimistically, 'All right then, here goes ...'

The locked side window exploded with a crash as he brought the barrel of the gun down on it hard.

No briefcase containing an asbestos firefighting suit.

For an awful moment, until he read the registration slip in the glove box, Auden thought Spencer had led him to the wrong car *again.*

*

In the labyrinth of cellars below the foyer of the hotel, Chief Fire Safety Officer George Bell paused attentively.

There was the faintest smell of petrol. Getting down to his knees, he put his ear against the ground. There was only the reverberation of the traffic in the street outside. He glanced back at the service elevator.

He sniffed.

There was a metal door at the end of the main cellar corridor with a legend painted on it in English and Chinese reading KEEP OUT.

Sniffing again, he went towards it, opened the door and,

glancing back to make sure no one was around, went inside.

There was a short length of rope on the floor of the little room and he used it to tie the door shut, secure against intruders.

It was 4.43 p.m., and starting at 7.10 a.m. that morning, in the course of less than ten short hours, The Spaceman had murdered three people.

Starting at 5.08 p.m. in the course of ten even shorter minutes, unless things changed drastically for the better, he would kill three more.

*

In the foyer of the hotel, Superintendent Ashwood shook his head and said, 'Bullshit! What forty five million dollars?' He looked around the foyer and saw only a throng of people at the front desk and the last of the firemen poking at the carpet with their fire extinguishers and axes, 'What do you think this is: some second rate bloody escapade about bloody sunken Nazi gold? Maybe some of those guys there at the desk drivelling about their precious film cans might be able to raise forty five million dollars for their next bloody Star Wars Six, but they sure as shit don't carry it around with them!' He thought of George Bell, 'I don't give a damn whether it's forty five million dollars or forty five million bloody doughnuts, Bell just isn't involved!' Auden and Spencer appeared at the main entrance, Auden settling his gun under his coat in its shoulder holster, and Ashwood, seeing Feiffer shake his head quickly in their direction, called out, 'You! Come here!'

Spencer, looking startled, said quickly, 'No, it's registered to George Bell. Honest!'

Ashwood said, 'What is registered to George Bell?' He turned to Feiffer with fire in his eyes, 'You've been searching his bloody car, haven't you?'

126

Spencer said, 'We only broke one window. It was locked—'

Auden shook his head, 'No briefcase.' He saw Ashwood's face and thought for an awful moment he might be from Internal Affairs, 'Are you with—'

Feiffer said evenly, 'This is Superintendent Ashwood of the Anti-Triad Bureau. He's here to look out for Mr Bell—whatever the rights and wrongs of the matter might be.'

Ashwood said, 'You're damned right about that!'

'Then where the hell is he?'

'He's in the hotel! If that's where the fire was then that's where he is!'

'Then why don't I see him?'

'Because he doesn't bloodywell have to report to you, that's why you don't see him!' He saw Auden settle the gun again, 'You touch that gun under your coat one more time, sonny, and I'll take it away from you and wrap it around your fucking ears!' (Auden said, 'Oh yeah? Oh, bloody yeah?')

Ashwood said, 'Yeah!'

Feiffer said evenly, 'No one's going to shoot Bell whatever he's done—'

'And what has he done?'

'At the moment, nothing. I just want to talk to him about a few things—like a missing firefighting suit.' Feiffer said firmly, 'Listen, Jack, I don't know Bell as well as you do – or as well as other people seem to – but I'm not prepared to let him out of the picture just because you say so. All I know for sure is that The Spaceman is dressed in a firefighting suit, Bell has one checked out to him that I can only assume he's got with him, he isn't where he's supposed to be, and, from the fact that you're here looking out for his interests, that he's quite probably somewhere here in this bloody hotel!'

'I'm here because—' Ashwood said abruptly, 'All right.

He is here. One of my people keeping an eye out for the Yakuza saw him drive up and he rang me, but that's as far as it goes. If your coppers saw him wandering about before the fire for all I know he could have been here to make a reservation for his little old granny!' Ashwood said, 'You find this bastard Wong, that's what you should be doing!'

'As a matter of fact, I already have.' Feiffer said to Auden, 'You and Bill go up to the fifth floor and find O'Yee and spread out into the corridors and see if you can locate Bell.' He saw Ashwood's face, 'And you, *sir,* oblige me by staying here!' He said as an afterthought, 'Get O'Yee over here.' He saw Lam coming towards him with a happy grin on his face and called him over to ask him a question.

Lam said gleefully, 'I'm not nuts. It was Teddy Wong all the time.' He put his hand on Ashwood's shoulder and Ashwood shook him off. Lam said happily to Feiffer, 'I'm sane. I'm as sane as you are.'

Feiffer asked Lam a single question.

The answer came back in numbers.

The second number was 512.

*

In Room 512, Teddy Wong waited behind the door with the knife in his hand. His knees were trembling. They felt weak. He put his hand on the door handle and tested it to see it was still locked, then went across to the bed to sit down on it. The curtains and the windows were open and he went across the room quickly and locked them, then took the typhoon bar from under the bed and bolted it across the glass and pulled the curtains.

Dirty, double-crossing—

He thought for a moment he was going to throw up.

The bathroom door was open. He went across and closed it and turned off the light.

Dirty double-crossing— He began to lose his resolve and wanted to hold his head in his hands and weep. His chest itched and then, in nervous sympathy, both his shoulder-blades. He clutched at his shirt and twisted it. He looked around for a way The Spaceman could get in and found nothing.

He went across to the bathroom, opened the door, and constantly listening, stood urinating into the toilet in the dark with his head turning back to the open bathroom door. He was frightened. The heavy knife kept getting damp with perspiration.

He zipped himself up, went to flush the toilet, and then, afraid of the noise, went into the room and closed the bathroom door behind him with a click.

Nowhere to hide.

He thought he saw the curtains move. There was a light inside the bathroom and then a sound, and then it was gone. Wong's fists started opening and closing spasmodically on the haft of the knife.

He heard a muffled footfall outside the door and then a sound as if something leaned against the door knob and tested it. The curtains moved. He heard the metal typhoon bar on the window groan, and then a sound from the closed bathroom.

Wong said, 'Oh God, oh God, oh God ...'

Whimpering, he got himself onto the bed and rolled up like a ball, his knife digging again and again into the mattress as he waited to be killed.

Wong glanced at his watch and then, its very existence on his body terrifying and disgusting him, ripped it off and threw it as far away as he could against the unmoving heavy curtain on the window.

4.57 p.m. The watch, an expensive product of the best Japanese silicon chip engineering, not inconvenienced in the slightest, went on ticking away as if nothing had happened.

129

*

In the locked room off the cellars, Bell said in a gasp, *'No—!'*

It wasn't possible. He had to be wrong. No one could seriously contemplate— He had to be wrong.

There were two forty gallon drums of petrol stored in the little room, fuel for the emergency generator. He put his fingers on the first drum's cap and opened it.

He checked the second drum.

The drums contained The Spaceman's total supply of petrol, and it had all gone – all eighty gallons of it.

Bell put his hand to his forehead in disbelief and said, *'No ...!'*

*

Wong, his hands on his temples a few feet from the locked door, shouted, 'Please! Please! It doesn't matter!' He heard a shuffling sound outside the door and then a rattle at the knob. *'Please!* I've got a knife! I swear I'll kill you before you can fire! *Please!'* His head was thumping, pulsing like a balloon. He clenched his hands to his head and shouted out inside the vault of his skull, 'Please! I don't care! I'll forget it! Tell them I'll forget it!' He knew the Yakuza. 'I'll forget it! I won't say anything! I don't care about the money! *Please!'*

He thought he saw the door begin to pulse in time to his temples as, on the other side, The Spaceman applied his gun like a blow lamp and, bit by bit, cut through the layers of varnish and wood and veneer to get to him. The wood was warping, coming alive. Wong shrieked, 'You bastard, you burned all my money!'

The knob rattled like a bell-less clapper. Wong shouted, 'You burned all my money!'

The knife was by him on the floor. He snatched it up.

He heard an explosion in his brain and then suddenly everything became cool and fresh and clear. Wong said, 'You burned all my money and I'm going to kill you for it.' The door wasn't warping at all. He saw that. It wasn't warping. There was no fire left. The Spaceman had run out of petrol and he was just standing there not knowing what to do while he, Wong, with a knife in his hand—

Wong shouted at the very rim of his sanity, 'You bastard, I'm going to cut your heart out!' wrenched open the door, and, in a sudden, all consuming explosion of chaos and darkness and pain, thought in that instant that somehow, for some totally unaccountable reason, the hotel had collapsed on top of him and he was dead.

13

On the sixth floor, Auden said with wide eyes, 'Jesus Christ, Boss, what the hell did you hit him with—an axe?' Blood was flowing copiously from Wong's face and he skipped to one side to avoid stepping in it.

'I hit him with a gun butt. He was coming at me with that thing.' The huge knife was lying slightly to one side of the open door to Room 512. Feiffer called out to Spencer searching the interior, 'Anything?'

'Nothing.' Spencer came out holstering his revolver and stepped into the blood, 'We'd better get him downstairs so someone can look at him.' Spencer said, 'Doctor Macarthur was downstairs talking to a film producer. I told him to get a room ready on my way up.' He looked down at Wong, 'Is he The Spaceman?'

'He thought *I* was. He thought I'd come to kill him.'

Auden made a whistling sound, 'It looks like he wasn't far wrong!' He caught the look on Feiffer's face and said quickly, 'Sorry. It's just a broken nose—'

Feiffer said, 'Pick him up.'

Auden glanced down at the blood, 'Unless you've bashed his septum into the frontal lobe of his brain—'

'I'll bash a septum into the frontal lobe of your brain if you don't pick him up!' Feiffer took the man under the armpits and ordered Spencer, 'Get the elevator door open. I want to get him downstairs before anyone dressed in a spacesuit decides it's accomplice killing time.'

He asked Spencer, 'Where did Macarthur say to put him?'

Spencer pressed the button by the elevator and the doors opened first time, 'Lam's office.' Spencer asked, 'How did you know he was here?'

'Five eleven and five twelve were Kong and Wu's rooms – the producers in the Palm Court. They were the only rooms empty in the entire place.' Feiffer ordered the hesitating Auden, 'Pick him up. His bloody feet aren't bleeding!' Wong made a groaning sound, 'I want to get him somewhere where we can talk to him before he realises what's going on.' He lifted Wong up and got blood on his hands and shirt cuffs and snapped at Auden, 'Not by the toes—hold him under the knees!' There was a *ping* and the service elevator at the other end of the corridor came up to floor level, 'Bill—!'

Spencer had his gun out again. The service elevator opened and there was nobody there. Spencer said, 'Nothing.' The main elevator door banged closed and then opened again. Spencer said, 'Come on, bring him down here!' He called out to Auden, 'Watch out, you're going to drop him!'

'He's covered in blood and—'

Feiffer said, 'Auden!'

'All right, all right!' The service elevator banged shut and he almost let go of Wong to reach for his gun. Spencer came forward and the main elevator door slammed closed and made an electronic *ping* as it went down to the next floor.

Feiffer yelled, 'Will you hold that bloody elevator!'

Spencer pushed at the buttons. Wong made a groaning noise and Auden, expecting a fountain of blood, said, 'Ugh!' and almost jerked the unconscious man from Feiffer's grasp.

The elevator door opened again and Lam said, 'You got him! You got Wong!' He started to come out of the elevator with murder in his eyes and Spencer pushed him in the centre of the chest and warned him, 'Keep away. He's unconscious.'

'Then beat him awake!' There was an iron bar in Lam's hand and he advanced again towards Spencer with it menacingly, 'Drop him on the ground and I'll smash the truth out of him!'

Spencer reached forward and took the iron bar. Feiffer and Auden, like a pair of kidnappers, had their unconscious bundle almost to the door of the elevator. Spencer said, 'You can do more good if you help us get him downstairs.'

'Why not just drop him down the liftshaft?' Lam said with ferocious malice, 'I'll be your witness. He tried to escape and he fell down trying to—'

Feiffer said, 'Shut up and hold that door open!' The service elevator made another pinging noise. Wong made a groaning sound and flickered his eyes open for a moment and Feiffer snapped at him, 'The Spaceman – is it Bell? *Is it George Bell?*'

Wong said, 'Oh!' and then groaned again as Auden dumped his end of him on the floor of the elevator.

Feiffer said urgently, 'Forty five million dollars—what was Jensen Ho talking about when he said you were after forty five million dollars?'

Spencer pushed Wong's feet a little farther into the elevator and pressed the DOWN button for the ground floor. Spencer, glancing at Wong's eyes, said with concern, 'He may be concussed. It sometimes happens with a blow to the face—'

'It was his bloody nose, not his face!' Feiffer got down on his knees and put his face six inches from the heavily breathing Wong, 'The Spaceman—' Wong made a moaning sound. 'It's no good. He hasn't the faintest idea what's happening.'

Auden said professionally, 'In the old days when the Chicago cops used to use rubber hoses—'

Spencer said warningly, 'Harry, Superintendent Ashwood is waiting downstairs. I think if we're going to hear that it's George Bell it might be an idea if Mr Ashwood's present together with an independent witness and—'

'Why? Because he's the bravest man you ever knew?' (Spencer said, 'Pardon?') 'What everyone seems to have forgotten around here is that The Spaceman's killed three people and for all I know intends to kill a couple of dozen more!'

'I just meant—' The elevator lights on the overhead panel went through floors three, two and one and Spencer said gratefully, 'We're almost there.'

'I want this man talking.'

Auden said, 'Yeah, right. We'll check that his septum isn't dislodged, and then caution him and then—'

'I want him talking now. The Spaceman is still loose in the hotel somewhere and unless we find him in the next few hours the powers-that-be in their wisdom are going to evacuate the place and quite probably supply him with enough people milling about in the street and in the foyer to keep him spraying petrol until Christmas.' He glanced at Lam, 'I don't want Ashwood in your office when we question him. If it's Bell I want to know about it without counsel for the defence shouting that it's all lies, damned lies and bloody statistics.' He saw Wong wince with pain and said in an undertone, 'This bastard's awake. He knows what we're saying and he's just biding his time to work out the best deal he can get.' The elevator reached the ground floor and the doors opened and Feiffer said to Auden, 'Pick him up!' saw O'Yee, Doctor Macarthur, Ashwood, what looked like half the guests in the hotel and all of the Hong Kong Fire Service waiting there, and ordered, 'Christopher, clear these people out of the way.' His eyes settled momentarily on Superintendent Ashwood, 'And I mean everybody.' He saw Auden offer Wong's knees to O'Yee and be refused. 'Bill, you go first and check Lam's office.' He moved forward and Macarthur bent down over Wong and touched at his nose exploratorily with a long boney finger.

Macarthur said to Wong cheeringly in the midst of all the anxiety and excitement, 'Don't worry, I'll look after you.' He saw the faintest flicker of recognition in the bleeding man's eyes.

Macarthur smiled reassuringly, 'Yes, that's right. You're in my hands now. I'm Doctor Macarthur—you know, from the Morgue.' He said in his best bedside manner, 'Oh dear, you don't look well at all ...'

*

It was a last resort. The Spaceman said aloud to himself, *'Damn it!'* and entered the main kitchen from the foyer and checked around in case there was anybody working in there. With room service being supplied from the smaller snack kitchens by the elevators, the main kitchen was deserted, and, with all the stoves and hot plates turned off, smelling of cold grease and disinfectant.

The Spaceman listened for a moment and heard the whirring of an exhaust fan working. The airconditioning, on the orders of the Fire Brigade, had been turned off after the first fire in the Palm Court and The Spaceman crossed the shining tiled floor and peered into a grille set at waist level in the far wall.

He touched carefully at the four screws holding the grille in its frame. Each of them still had a human hair lying across the slots and he nodded to himself in satisfaction, took out a small penknife from his pocket and prised the grille loose.

The grille was part of the main utilities duct serving the ground, first and second floors. The Spaceman squeezed inside and pulled the grille tight against its jamb behind him, the dummy wooden screws giving the appearance that the grille was screwed in tight.

Ten feet along the dark metal tunnel was his suit and gun. The Spaceman took his key ring out of his pocket and, pointing it ahead down the abyss, flicked on the tiny flashlight attached to it and illuminated the passage.

He paused for a moment, running through the diagram of the tunnels in his mind, then, deciding, began crawling towards the junction of three pipes where, if he stood up carefully with his head and shoulders up in the pipe going to the first floor, he could assemble his gun and dress.

He passed a grille opening into one of the bars off the rear of the main ground floor foyer and shone his light down onto the wall behind it.

Like all modern buildings, it looked as if the wall was made out of cardboard. He touched the construction, being careful not to shine the light through the grille into the bar.

He rested his hand flat against the wall and exerted measured pressure. The wood veneer tiles and thin cement bricks creaked slightly.

One good push and they would collapse into the bar like a door opening in a wall. The Spaceman had a cellophane wrapped bag of plastic explosive tied by a string to the muzzle of his petrol gun, copper mercury detonators and fuses attached to it in a matchbox by tape.

He undid the bag and, pulling loose an ounce of the explosive with his fingers, primed it with a detonator and left the matchbox and the main charge on the floor of the airconditioning pipe.

He would not need the main charge until later. He could collect it on the way back.

Crawling along an airconditioning tunnel was a last resort, but he forced himself not to hurry.

The tunnel was slightly dirty with neglect and he had a special reason for wanting to keep his clothes clean and uncreased.

It was 5.07 p.m. and The Spaceman, reaching the

junction, dressed quickly in his suit and assembled his gun in a series of rapid, well practised clicks.

*

They were getting nothing. In Lam's office Feiffer snapped at Macarthur, 'If you give him an injection I'll never get anything out of him!'

'The man's in pain!' Macarthur said hopelessly, 'I don't even know if he's conscious! I'm a pathologist, not a—'

Wong was lying full length on Lam's desk, his face ashen.

Feiffer shook the man by the shoulders and said urgently, 'Wong, is it Bell?' For all he knew, even now, The Spaceman could be— He grasped Wong by the face and shook him back and forth to get a response, 'For God's sake, man—*is The Spaceman George Bell?*'

*

In the cellars, Bell said, 'Oh my God ...!'

It was unbelievable, impossible. He was outside the generator room staring at something on the wall of a corridor.

Bell said again, 'Oh my God!'

He heard the service elevator at the far end of the corridor open and a voice shout out loudly in Cantonese, 'They've caught The Spaceman—it's that insurance fellow Wong. They've got him in the manager's office—' and Bell shouted out, 'No, it isn't him! It couldn't be! It's—' He saw the thing on the wall again, *'NO!'* He rushed down the corridor, almost colliding with two cleaners leaning on their brooms and, trying the elevator and finding it stopped on another floor, tore open the door to the stairs and took them two at a time, racing for the foyer.

*

In the foyer, O'Yee said casually to Mukherjee, 'By the way, I don't suppose you happen to have any spare—'

Mukherjee's attention was focussed, like Shimada's, on the door to the manager's office. Mukherjee said irritably, 'What?'

*

Ashwood yelled, 'George!' He saw Bell rushing towards him, 'George, what the hell are you—'

Bell yelled, 'Get out! Get out!' He burst through a knot of film producers and sent them scattering, crashed past O'Yee and knocked him to the ground, saw O'Yee recognise him and start to reach for his gun and punched the weapon from the man's hand, still running, 'Get out for Christ's sake!' Ashwood caught him around the chest and he jerked his elbow and caught the man a stunning blow across the jaw and broke free, 'Get out, Jack! Jack—!'

The office door came open and Auden said, 'What the hell's going on—?' a moment before Bell caught him by the shoulder and in one motion seemed to launch him out into the foyer. Spencer was a little behind, looking surprised. Bell grabbed him in a stranglehold and, pivoting, hurled him out after Auden onto the ground. Bell burst into the room and shouted, 'Out! Get everybody out of the hotel!' There was a shattering detonation from inside the bathroom as The Spaceman blew out a section of the wall with plastic explosive and Bell said, '*Oh my God—!*'

Feiffer said, 'What the hell was—' He got to the bathroom door and wrenched at the knob to get it open, reaching in under his coat for his gun. Bell had Macarthur around the waist and was literally half carrying the man out of the room. From inside the bathroom there was another deeper report as The Spaceman got his feet against the remaining section of wall and ventilator grille and pushed it hard into the room to make a door. The entire wall was collapsing. There was another crash and the airconditioning grille and the masonry around it burst in a shower of white masonry dust.

On the foyer floor, Spencer had his gun out, bringing it up to get in a shot. He saw Ashwood's shape loom over him for a second and turned to say, 'No, I'll shoot him in the legs—' as Ashwood yelled, 'No, don't fire!' and kicked his pistol as hard as he could out of Spencer's grasp. Spencer said, surprised, 'No, you shouldn't have—' as Auden got his Python up, swung it like a sword against Ashwood's ankles and scythed him down to the floor.

At the bathroom door, Feiffer said, 'God Almighty—!' The Spaceman was coming out of the wall, like something from a nightmare. Bell got his fingers around Feiffer's shirt collar, twisted hard to get a good grip, and, wrenching hard, pulled him off his feet, seemed somehow to catch him as he overbalanced, and shoved him out of the door.

By Wong, Macarthur said, 'Oh dear—' He ducked as Bell rushed towards him and ran out of the open office door, collided with Auden weaving the Python to get a shot in, fell over the top of him and said, 'Oh, dear oh, dear—'

The Spaceman was in the open bathroom shaking his head, bringing his gun up to find a target. Lam said, 'No—!' The gun was moving, searching.

Untangling himself from Macarthur, Auden shouted, 'Goddammit!' There was a whiplash crack from next to him as Feiffer tried to get a shot in at The Spaceman through the impossible angle of the open bathroom door and Auden, snap-aiming his Python, got off a magnum round that blew a chunk of wood out of the office door jamb and deafened everyone around him.

Wong was up on his elbow, the blood flowing freely from his nose again. He saw Anthony Lam transfixed in terror beside him. Wong said, 'Anthony—'

Bell's eyes were travelling up and around the room,

looking for something. Another magnum round from Auden's gun ripped a chunk of masonry from the wall behind him and then there was another, sharper shot as Feiffer fired again at The Spaceman and missed.

The Spaceman seemed to be shaking his head. Bell's eyes travelled past him and out into the foyer. He took a step towards the office door, still looking for something. Bell said, 'You dirty—'

Lam shouted to The Spaceman, *'No! Don't!'*

It was a babble, all happening at the same time.

Ashwood. Bell saw Ashwood looking at him. Ashwood said, 'George—!' Bell saw Ashwood shake his head. For an instant he saw Ashwood mouth the words, 'Not twice, I can't stop them twice—' and then, suddenly, Bell had a strange look on his face, almost as if— He seemed to be stopped in time, like a photograph, smiling at Ashwood with a sad smile.

The Spaceman's gun behind him made a clicking noise, and Bell, still smiling, tears forming in his eyes, looked up at something outside in the foyer, seemed to sigh, and then – to Ashwood's sudden horror – shut the door.

The Spaceman's gun was dribbling flame from its nozzle and Bell shook his head at him in something approaching a terrible disappointment and, holding the office door shut, stood with his forehead against it, and closed his eyes.

The Spaceman, contained in the box of the bathroom, was standing in a growing sea of flame. From out of that flame, there came a single jet of boiling searing flame that, in an instant, turned the room and everything in it to lava.

He was the bravest man that a great number of people had ever known, and when Feiffer and Ashwood finally managed to enter the burned out room there was nothing left of either him, Lam or Wong but a single gold, unengraved signet ring which, for some reason known only to the manufacturer, had not burned.

14

At 7.08 p.m., as a precursor to the possible evacuation of the hotel, the Fire Brigade began bringing tenders into Empress of India Street and connecting their hoses to hydrants to check available pressure.

A foam wagon stood by in the rear carpark, the officers manning it glancing up at the night sky and the brightly lit six storey hotel tower in front of them.

There was a freshening wind blowing in from the sea. A fireman lit an unwanted cigarette nervously and blew the smoke in the direction of the flashing blue light on his engine.

Serially, the warm night wind was increasing in intensity.

15

On the phone in the Detectives' Room, Feiffer said provocatively, 'And just what do you propose to do then? Evacuate the entire district? I've been talking to some of the firemen out there and they say they have about as much chance of confining the fire to the hotel as you'd have confining a tiger to a dog kennel. This isn't New York or London. Most of the buildings in Hong Bay are old and tinder dry, and they don't have fire doors.' He paused for a moment, considering the awful possibility of it, 'Not two streets away there's a complex of government resettlement blocks housing no less than – at the most conservative estimate – four or five thousand people. You might have seen it – it's covered in clothes lines on every floor holding – in this warm weather – very dry washing. Have you any idea just what—'

The Commander said evenly, controlling himself, 'Harry, I don't have any idea at all. None. The only idea I have is that I've got tourists to think of.'

'You start evacuating tourists and you'll have the biggest non-tourist riot on your hands since the Boxer Rebellion.' Feiffer said quietly, convincingly, 'Neil, the reason we haven't had a panic is that the Chinese know the tourists *haven't* been evacuated, so they assume, just because of what you've been saying, that if the tourists are safe, so are they. You try and start a little evacuation by class and status in this town and you just won't believe what'll happen. And the last thing we need is to have the Riot Squad shooting tear gas and rubber bullets around the place while half the city is in flames and the important people are taking to the boats. And apart from anything else, we haven't got enough boats.'

The Commander said after a pause, 'Then you'd better find The Spaceman or whatever he calls himself—and pretty damn quick.'

'He doesn't call himself anything. That's half the problem. If I at least knew what the hell he was supposed to represent I'd be a little further advanced than I am. At the moment I'm nowhere.' O'Yee was at his desk following the conversation and making notes on his pad and shaking his head, 'All I've got so far is that he's a man who likes shooting a gasoline gun off in a hotel. What I had before was that the Singapore owners of the hotel wanted the place burned to the ground for profit – but that turns out to be nonsense, then what I had was that it was the Triads – and that turned out, similarly, to be more nonsense.' There was silence on the line, 'Then I had the fact that The Green Slime here was employed by Teddy Wong to open the case containing the million dollars and that – since The Spaceman burned the money to cinders – also turned out to be—'

'And now Wong's dead.'

'And now Wong's dead.'

There was another pause and then the Commander said, 'And then you had George Bell.'

'I still haven't found his firefighting suit. I've got Spencer and Auden over at the hotel searching the airconditioning tunnels, but I'm still—' Feiffer paused and then went on before the man could protest, 'I'm still not totally convinced that Bell is out of it.'

'You said earlier that Ashwood of the Triad Bureau told you the Yakuza had been seeing Wong.'

'Wong happens to be dead. The Spaceman killed him.'

'He also killed George Bell!'

'I know he did! What I don't understand is why George Bell fought his way to get behind a closed door so he *could* kill him! The way people like Wong and Lam seem to have been telling it it all reeks of a series of nasty little intrigues and double crosses, and for all I know Bell could have been just as involved as—'

'You told me George got everyone out!'

'I'm not denying it. What I don't understand—'

'Bell got everyone out because he was that sort of man! He was the sort of man who thought less of his own skin than of—'

'I just don't understand why he shut that bloody door, that's all!'

'In order to save you—why else?'

'We were already outside! There was enough gunfire starting to kill twenty bloody Spacemen! All Bell had to do was stand to one side and we could have filled The Spaceman full of so many holes he would have looked like a sieve. Instead, he chose to shut the goddamned door in our faces so The Spaceman could shoot off his little gun in the comfort and confinement of—'

'I won't have it, Harry! I may have to agree with what you say about evacuating the hotel, but when it comes to slandering a man like George Bell I just won't have it! Not a bit of it!'

'He wasn't bloody Mahatma Gandhi! From what I gather when he was investigated by ICAC the main reason he was found whiter than white was that he was broke! Isn't it possible that one day he got a bit tired of being the Knight Of The Holy Grail and decided to take a few dollars for himself? God knows if the Japanese Yakuza was involved there would have been enough money around to tempt anybody!'

'You said it was Wong who was involved with the Yakuza!'

'Ashwood said that, not me. And Ashwood was Bell's friend.' Feiffer said reasonably, 'Look, Neil, I'm not trying to turn Bell into the number one villain, all I'm trying to say is that the one time we had The Spaceman within shooting range, Bell, almost on cue, appeared from nowhere to protect him—'

'Are you telling me that George Bell was the sort of man to give up his life to help a homicidal *psycho?*'

'I don't think The Spaceman is a psycho. I think he's got a very sane plan in mind and the only trouble is that I don't seem to be able to find out what it is.' He glanced again at O'Yee. 'The fact that The Green Slime knew who was threatening him – Teddy Wong – suggests to me that once they'd used his services they were going to bump him off. Since Wong wasn't The Spaceman The Spaceman must have been sane enough to convince Wong at least that there was some profit in the killing. When I spoke to Wong he didn't seem surprised that a street sweeper and a couple of producers had been incinerated: he only seemed concerned to keep feeding me his cock and bull story about Lam losing his mind. If The Spaceman could convince someone as basically tough as Wong then I fail to see just how he could have been—'

'He convinced Wong about the million dollars—then he burned it! That's why Wong ran. You said he had a knife—who the hell was that for? Bloody Santa Claus?'

'The Spaceman double crossed him! The million dollars didn't count. Maybe the forty five million come-on designed to terrify The Slime by its mere enormity wasn't a come-on at all and it really exists. Maybe the million in the case was Wong's *pay* and once The Slime was out of it and the case couldn't be broached—'

'Wong *insured* the bloody money!'

'And the moment it had been stolen and the hotel burned to the ground, Wong, who had more debts to ex-wives and money-lenders than goddamned Howard

146

Hughes had Mormons—would have had himself declared bankrupt, and shoved his cool million into a Swiss bank account, been offered the manager's job in the rebuilt Yakuza hotel, and lived happily ever after!'

'Bullshit!' The Commander said, 'Any idea that George Bell was involved in something like this is a load of bloody bullshit!'

'Then where the hell's his firefighting suit? And if he was in the hotel when the money was burned *why didn't he appear to help put out the fire?*'

'Because he wasn't *in* the hotel!'

'He was seen by my two Constables!' Feiffer said abruptly, 'Listen, Neil, somewhere in that hotel there's something worth forty five million dollars and that's what The Spaceman is after. I think he may have been employed in the first place by the Yakuza and Wong to get the million and burn down some of the hotel so they could take it over, but now I have a feeling he's got his own little football in his hands and, having eliminated Wong and anyone else in the place who might have stopped him at the twenty yard line, I think he's running with it.'

'What the hell's worth forty five million dollars? Nothing's worth forty five million dollars! What are you talking about: a ton and a half of bloody gold bullion? And even if he gets it, what's he going to do with it—take it out on a fire engine?' The Commander said before Feiffer could answer, 'I used to be on the streets myself, Harry, I wasn't born in a Commander's uniform, so don't try and tell me it's heroin or something. That much heroin – even in its purest form possible – would still represent a parcel weighing almost three hundred pounds. If the Yakuza were bringing that much heroin into Hong Kong the bloody Triads would be keeping them out with goddamned machine guns and negotiating with the Palestine Liberation Front to buy bloody guided missiles! And if it's heroin, what the hell is it doing being brought into Hong Kong

147

in the first place? People would be trying to get it out!'

'I didn't say it was heroin.'

'Then what? *The bloody British Crown Jewels?* The British Crown Jewels would be in the hotel safe and your man Jensen Ho – The Green Slime – would be busy cracking that and not some plastic box holding paper money.' The Commander said with heavy sarcasm, 'I suppose you have checked what's in the safe? I hate to spoil your theories of the exotic, but—'

Feiffer said evenly, 'The safe has got nothing of value in it. Hotel staff always have to view the contents of packages to be put in the safe before they'll accept them – for the insurance – and the total value of the stuff in the Empress of India's safe comes to about ten thousand dollars. There are a few jewelled cuff links, papers and film gear, a couple of thousand dollars worth of U.S. and Hong Kong travellers' cheques, business papers, a few—'

'Who put the stuff in the safe?'

'Lam.'

'Then if Lam was involved maybe there was something he didn't make out a receipt for and—'

'Lam wasn't involved. Lam was the patsy. If he'd been involved and he'd put something in the safe worth stealing, why the hell didn't he just take it out again and steal it? Spacemen and big spectacular productions for the sake of it only happen in the movies. If there was something worth having in the safe why not just—'

'So what the hell are you doing?'

'What I'm doing is the only thing I can do! I'm trying to find out what Bell—'

'It wasn't Bell! Bell is dead!'

'Then where the hell's his missing firefighting suit? It's not in the bloody ducts because we've checked!'

'I don't know! I don't know where his firefighting suit is and I don't – even after talking to you – know any more about what's going on in that hotel than I did before!' The

Commander said with disgust, 'Goddamned wooden flying saucers and people dressed up as Frankenstein and Boris Karloff – that isn't police work – it all sounds like something out of a bloody science fiction film!' At the other end of the line Feiffer paused for a moment as something failed to make a connection in his mind. The Commander said, 'And Harry, that Slime character and his story about forty five million dollars, I can tell you free of charge—'

Feiffer said, 'Yeah?'

The Commander said vehemently, 'In my opinion—it's bullshit!'

*

In the generator room in the cellars, Auden turned his back to Spencer so Spencer could brush the dust and cobwebs from his coat, glanced carefully around the room to make sure there were no airconditioning ducts, steam pipes, dumb waiters or other traps for the unwary crawler in a recently dry-cleaned best suit and said with a sniff, 'Why doesn't Harry Feiffer go crawling around the bloody airconditioning pipes? Why always me?' His valet paused for a moment to answer and Auden jerked his head back over his shoulder and said, 'The sleeve, you missed the sleeve.'

'Harry's the senior officer, Phil.' Spencer found a heavy concentration of black soot from one of the pipes, waved his hand in front of it to see if it would loose itself by pure incantation, found it would not, and took out his clean white handkerchief and brushed it away. Spencer said, 'You know, we're the troops. The job of a senior officer, according to the manual—' He glanced around the sleeve for more dirt, looked down with regret at his handkerchief and said brightly, 'That's done. You're clean again. The manual says—'

The petrol driven emergency generator had a piece of rope lying across it. Auden picked it up and twisted it into

149

a garotte, looked around the room for somewhere to put it and tossed it into a corner of the room by two forty gallon drums, 'What the hell did he close the door for? If he'd left it open I could have got a shot in.' The rope looked untidy and he went forward, picked it up and, for somewhere neat to put it, handed it to Spencer.

Spencer said charitably, 'Maybe he was trying to save us, Phil.'

'Well, he sure wasn't trying to save himself, was he?' Auden took the rope back and put it on top of one of the drums. 'What the hell are we supposed to be looking for anyway?' He demanded, 'Do you think those two bloody idiot cleaners knew what they were talking about? About Bell being in here?' He picked up the rope again and went forward and hooked the cord over the handles of the door, found if he tied it it kept the door closed from the inside, and asked, 'What's the point of locking yourself in a generator room? That's just crazy!'

'Maybe he was looking for something.' Spencer went forward to the drums, 'Petrol, maybe.'

'He could have got as much as he wanted from The Spaceman!' Auden said suddenly intimately, 'Listen, I heard that Bell was some sort of hero in Viet Nam or somewhere: that he saved a whole lot of people's lives. Is it possible a guy like that – if he was only in it for the money—' He seemed a little embarrassed, 'I got the impression that he was—' He shrugged, 'You know, well—*religious.*' He looked at Spencer for a cackle of sarcastic laughter.

Spencer said, 'Really? I didn't know you knew him.'

'I didn't. I just—' Auden said quickly, 'I saw him at the door, you know, when he must have known he was going to get the chop and—' He kicked the first drum with his shoe and said before the sound came, 'Petrol and goddamned plenty if you want it.' Auden said irritably, 'I don't know, do I?'

150

The drum made an empty ringing sound.

Auden said, 'That's funny.' He kicked the second drum, 'They're both empty.' He furrowed his brow and looked at the generator tank, 'You don't think Bell was down here loading up on ...' He said quickly, 'Nah, it must be in the generator engine tank.'

Spencer, interested, said, 'What, you saw a cross around his neck or something?'

'Of course I didn't see a cross around his neck or something! People don't wear crosses around their necks these days!' He looked at Spencer suspiciously, 'Do they?' (Spencer said, 'No, I don't. Some people do though—') 'I just—' Auden said awkwardly, 'Well, he—well—well, he looked *up*—didn't he?'

'Did he?'

'Yeah! I was trying to get in a shot past him and I saw him and he had a sort of sick look on his face—you know, like those plaster saints you see outside churches – you know—' Auden put on a dyspeptic eye-rolling look of sanctity— 'You know, *that sort of look!*' Auden said quickly, fixing his mind onto the more scientifically deducible truths of the world, 'What would you say that tank on the generator would hold? About eighty gallons? That's what the drums would hold.' He saw Spencer pondering something, 'Look, forget I mentioned it, all right? I just thought that if he was what everyone said he was then if he was religious then it'd be a bit better for his family. All right? I'm not going soft or anything, I just thought—' Auden said angrily, 'How the hell do I know? For all I know he could have just been looking at a fly on the bloody ceiling! For all I know he wasn't religious at all—what the hell do I know about bloody religion anyway?'

Spencer said quietly, 'It's certainly a very nice thought if you're right.'

'Yeah. Sure. Bloody lovely.' Auden snapped, 'Look, let's just check the bloody petrol tank and make sure the bloody

151

stuff's where it should be, O.K.? That's what the bloody manual says, isn't it?'

Spencer said encouragingly, 'It's a nice thought.'

'Yeah. So is bloody sarsaparilla and goddamned ice cream!' Auden whipped off the cap of the petrol tank, sniffed inside the nozzle, and, satisfied at the appropriate odour of hydrocarbons, gave the tank a blow with his foot and said before it connected, 'Full of petrol, just where it should be, full to the bloody gills with eighty gallons of high bloody octane super boom-boom quality bloody—'

The petrol tank on the emergency generator made a hollow ringing sound.

Auden, his attention to the Paradisal joys of the next world brought back to the menace of this one in an instant of sudden comprehension, said in a gasp, *'Hell—!'*

*

It was lovely, just like the War. In the foyer, the people had all gathered with their suitcases and they were sitting in the chairs and on the lounges and on the floor, talking quietly to each other and whispering. Some of them seemed to be praying.

Through the open door of the office came and went a steady stream of white coated Scientific officers, fingerprint men and people from the Fire Brigade.

Outside, the night was dark and warm and there were flashing lights and men in uniform moving about and gathering in little knots to confer and make plans. A few bedraggled monster suits lay in the corners of the foyer, discarded, and here and there, near them, fallen down placards advertising films and the last vestiges of peace.

At the front desk, the night manager, an anxious, dark haired girl from Israel, was flicking through papers, organising lists for evacuation, and talking to the bell boys and the maids.

152

Trays of steaming hot cups of coffee were being brought out from the hastily reopened kitchen, and pretty soon, there would be soup.

They had moved her piano down from upstairs into the centre of the foyer and Carole began for the second time since 7 p.m. her repertoire of wartime tunes: *The White Cliffs Of Dover, We'll Meet Again, Keep Smiling Through,* and the one her husband had liked best: *Together.*

It was lovely.

People were actually listening.

*

It was a little after 8 p.m. and, somewhere in the hotel, as the guests and staff waited for the evacuation that was not going to come, eighty gallons of petrol were missing.

Outside, in the street and in the rear carpark, the firemen and their officers, told of the news, shook their heads in the steadily freshening wind in from the sea and fell ominously silent.

16

The truth had come to him in whispers in the darkness. In the darkness The Spaceman had heard the whispered truths of the young and middle-aged and, louder, he had heard the dry rasping of the old – survivors from another generation – as they struggled to comprehend.

He had heard them behind him in the movies, heard the girl say in a gasp to her boyfriend, 'He's going to shoot her!' The middle-aged say with an affected yawn, 'Oh, sure, now they get marooned in space and there's a flying saucer that—' Heard the old say, 'I don't understand: why did he hire someone to murder his wife when he could have just divorced her?' Heard children say—

The whispers in the dark had told him. He had begun going to the cheaper seats to hear not the soundtrack, but the voices behind him interpreting reality.

'You watch, the convicts are going to break into a house, hold the woman hostage and get her husband to—'

'They're going to—'

'He's got a gun!'

'The monster's going to sit with the girl, you watch—and then she'll give him a flower and he'll go off and then—'

'Here goes the priest. He'll walk up to the space craft and they'll disintegrate him and then the tanks will start firing—'

'I know what's going to happen. What's going to happen is—'

'If that was me up there I know what I'd do ...'

'I know what I'd do—'

Reality. Successions of images run on the surface of the brain from childhood. Flickerings of a strange internal language, anticipations of actions from celluloid clues, pervasive propagandas for ethical and unethical behaviour, learned responses for artificial situations—

'If that ever happened to me in real life ...'

The Spaceman had made it real life.

Lam: intimations of madness courtesy of the psychiatric movie firm of Bette Davis and Joan Crawford. Wong: greed courtesy of every Big Job movie ever made with additions of *The Sting* and uninterrupted television effluvia of big business mechanisations and swindles. Jensen Ho: a simpler soul. The Convicts Have Your Family movies of the fifties. The Yakuza: *The Godfather*—a chance to make money to increase their empire when, in reality, all the empire could ever want would accrue from their capital invested safely in the nearest bank at ten percent base rate interest. The Spaceman himself—*The Beast Abroad*.

Every movie ever made on the subject proved that the world never came to an end, that the meteor never hit.

The hotel foyer across the road was full of people believing it.

George Bell ...

The innocent dupe sent to The Chair for a Crime He Did Not Commit.

Whispers, clues, reflections of reality, reality itself ...

The Spaceman, sitting in his car with the briefcase containing his asbestos suit next to him, smiled.

The Movies.

The only mistake he had made had been not to kill Wong earlier.

The Spaceman saw someone he knew crossing from the

155

hotel towards him and he got out of his car, still smiling, to say hullo.

*

In the Detectives' Room, making notes on his pad in an effort to avoid the disgusting spectacle of Auden eating noodles at the next desk, O'Yee said, 'Harry, this whole thing is beginning to sound to me like the plot of half a dozen classic movies rolled into one. The only thing it hasn't got so far is Humphrey Bogart in *Casablanca* walking off into the airport sunset with Claude Rains in the last reel.' He saw Feiffer glance up at him from his desk with a heavenward gazing look on his face and said quickly, 'No, I know I see everything through goddamn silver screen glasses, but you just try it out.' He looked at Spencer and found he had his interest. 'This business with the street cleaner: you think about it for a moment.' He stood up and held his hands out like a director calling for silence on the set, 'Here's this scene at dawn in a deserted street, right? Big hotel or building of some sort right by. A slight wind blowing papers around – no titles, no music, the audience all settled down with their popcorn bags unopened – and then pan to this fucking great flying saucer – gasp from audience – but they know it's a science fiction film, so gasp stops. We show that the flying saucer is made of plywood. The popcorn bags start rustling – then wham! here's this guy in a space suit standing next to it. End rustling. Hold that shot for a moment. Then, start music, there's a street sweeper or two wandering up the street – a bit of comic relief – only it isn't funny because we know—because it's film, that the the street sweepers are going, somehow, to get the chop—'

Auden said with a mouthful of noodles in his mouth, 'Crap!'

Auden was the sort of guy O'Yee always got behind in

the movies. O'Yee said automatically, 'Would you please be quiet. Thank you.' He raised his finger to show the scene was continuing, 'Then after a little bit of business, kapow! the Spaceman's real and he starts moving and—' O'Yee began shambling towards Spencer with his finger pointed like a gun, a glazed expression in his eyes.

Spencer said, 'Gosh, that's really good.'

'—and then, build up the tension so the audience is grasping the popcorn bag harder and harder and harder ... and then—whoosh! Out comes the fire and it envelops the poor old innocent street sweeper, covers the screen in fire, the fire rushes out at the audience, going all sorts of yellow and red and—and then: TITLES!'

Spencer said enthusiastically, 'I've seen that one! It was called—'

Auden said with a grunt, 'It was called every rotten movie you ever saw.'

Feiffer said to O'Yee, 'Go on.'

'And we call it *The Spaceman*. Right?' O'Yee turned to Auden with an accusing look in his eyes, 'Isn't that what everyone calls him? Why the hell not The Arsonist or the goddamned murderer or—'

That was an easy one. Auden said with a noodle on his chin, 'Because he's dressed in a fucking space suit, that's why!'

'Right! Why?'

'What do you mean "why"?' Auden said, 'Because he's—' He looked at Spencer, 'I don't know why. Because he needs protection from the flames?' He recovered quickly, 'Anyway it isn't a space suit, it's a firefighting suit that just happens to look like a space suit!'

Feiffer, his eyes on O'Yee, said slowly, 'Which is why, since it was a firefighting suit he stood next to a fire engine when he shot the sweeper.'

Auden said, 'I thought you said he stood next to a flying saucer.' He said, 'Oh.'

O'Yee said, 'And then, on the scene comes Lam and Wong. Lam is the respectable, vaguely neurotic type – let's call him Joan Crawford—'

Auden muttered, 'Shit,' saw O'Yee glare at him and pretended the reference was to the quality of the noodles.

Feiffer said, 'And Teddy Wong?'

'Bette Davis. And, in this movie, Bette Davis—'

Spencer said brightly, 'My mother used to watch those movies on late-night television. Bette Davis was always the rotten one and she wanted something from Joan Crawford – an inheritance or something – and she was always trying to convince the doctors and Joan Crawford herself that she was around the bend by, you know, tape recordings of dead relatives and—'

Feiffer said, 'And messages on windows and cigarettes and—'

O'Yee said triumphantly, 'Right!'

Spencer said quietly, 'Life mirroring art ...'

Auden muttered, 'What the hell does that mean?'

O'Yee rubbed his hands together, 'Right! And then those two film producers Kong and Wu get the chop in plain sight of everyone in the Palm Court Room—Jack the Ripper strikes in Victorian London. Then Shimada and Mukherjee get terrified out of their minds in their room and urged off downstairs into the foyer where the million dollars in the case—the Big Job movie. Goldfinger at Fort Knox, all the George Segal movies ever made – the old Nazi treasure in the lake bullshit – and then—'

Feiffer said, 'And then The Spaceman burns the money to ash. Why?'

O'Yee said, 'So Bette Davis, the rotten one, knows the truth, that someone else has it in for her – that there's a double cross – you know, that for example the doctor she's in cahoots with: the one feeding Joan Crawford the poison is secretly—'

Spencer said, 'You're saying that Wong had some sort of

158

deal going with The Spaceman concerning the million dollars—'

Feiffer said, 'And the Japanese Yakuza—'

'—to steal the million dollars—'

O'Yee said, 'Yeah. And The Green Slime. The poor honest Joe Doakes intimidated into helping because his family is in danger from the convicts—'

Auden said, 'I saw that one. It had that character who played Ben Casey on TV in it.' He looked at Spencer, 'You know, man, woman, birth, death, infinity ...' Spencer, not a great television watcher, met him with a blank look, 'You know, and then wham! the hospital doors fly open and in comes—' Auden said irritably, going back to his noodles in a funk, 'Aw, forget it!'

O'Yee said definitely, 'It's a whole lot of movie plots. It all sounds like—'

Feiffer, echoing the Commander's words, said quietly, 'Just like the plot of a sci fi movie ...'

'Like a whole mass of movies, Harry! Like every movie you ever saw!'

Feiffer said, 'And Bell?'

O'Yee said, 'I don't know.' He paused for a moment, 'Gary Cooper in *High Noon?*' He turned to Auden, 'That was the one where the townspeople all kicked Marshal Kane in the face and he was left to fight the bad guys alone and—'

Auden said, 'I've seen *High Noon!* What do you think I am? Everyone's seen *High Noon!*'

Feiffer said, 'If Bell was innocent.'

'If he wasn't why did he warn everyone in the office?'

Feiffer said, 'Maybe. If he was innocent, just who are the townspeople who kicked him in the face supposed to be? Us?'

'Maybe, yes!' O'Yee said in appeal, 'God Almighty, Harry, everyone who's ever met Bell claims he was the bravest man who ever lived. Maybe if everybody says it—'

159

Feiffer finished for him, 'Maybe it's just our dirty, suspicious little minds. Right?'

'Maybe. *Yes.*'

Feiffer, smiling faintly, said, 'O.K., O.K., so you're telling me the whole thing is a combination of what? *The Day The Earth Stood Still* or *Invasion Of The Martians, Hysteria* or whatever all those Davis Crawford films were called, *High* bloody *Noon* and—and what?'

'No, I think all that was just the sub plot that surrounds the thing.' O'Yee said with the easy criticism of a life long cineaste, 'No, I think whoever came up with all this sold it to people like Wong and the Yakuza and to a lesser extent The Green Slime because all these stories are so well known and so hackneyed as to be immediately recognisable as reality. When in fact they're not reality at all, but what people who have spent their lives going to movies and being influenced by them have come to think of as reality!' O'Yee said, 'It's like all this violence on television: if you spent all your childhood and life watching it you begin to think that the normal, the usual, the only method of dealing with any sort of slight emotional upset is to start drawing pistols and killing people.' O'Yee, in full flight, said, 'What I think is that The Spaceman has a really genuine, original idea of his own behind all this and he's only used the movie plots to sell the idea to the idiots he needed to help him with it.'

'Then why did he burn the money?'

'Because it didn't matter. The million dollars prize was straight out of a movie. What he really wanted—' Realising it, O'Yee said, 'Christ Almighty, how much more obvious can he get? Not only was the idea of taking the million in a glass case straight out of a movie – *Topkapi* or something – the goddamned money was movie money itself! It was the cost of ten minutes filming of a movie!'

'The elusive forty five million dollars.' Feiffer said, 'If the million was the prize Wong thought he was going to get—'

O'Yee said, 'According to what the Companies Squad and Ashwood told you, it's a fair bet that even if he didn't get that he would have got the managership of the Empress of India when the Yakuza took it over.'

'The Green Slime said Wong knew about the forty five million. He said he mentioned it.'

'Maybe he did.' O'Yee said, 'Maybe The Spaceman told Wong to say it.' He said quietly, 'That's from a movie too – and it's called *The Sting* – a little bit of fiction that makes the whole thing sound real, big and pointless to try and fight against. Only this time it wasn't a fiction!'

Auden said, 'How many fucking movies are there in this business?'

Feiffer said again, wearily, *'Then why did he burn the million dollars?'*

'To convince someone that the movie wasn't going the way the movie always went. That there wasn't a predictable end to it.' O'Yee said, 'Why the hell do you think all those movie people are sitting about in the foyer like a gang of good little boys and girls? They're not Londoners in the Blitz queuing up to go into the air raid shelters and waiting for goddamned Winston Churchill to tell them it's all their finest hour, they're Asians. By rights, they should be running amok, shouting and waving their arms about and looking for meat cleavers to use against the cops. Instead, they're psyched out.' O'Yee said, 'They're film producers! They're sitting there because, in the end, they've come to believe all their own conceits and because everything comes out all right in their end of their own movies they think—' O'Yee said with the smug grin of an insider, 'Can you think of anything more designed to convince a film man that someone's serious than burning *money?* No one does that—not even Marlon Brando!' O'Yee said definitively, 'The whole thing, the whole, planned, worked-out and played-out scenario is aimed at one thing – as a sort of public relations exercise to terrify only one group of people – the people in that hotel – the film people. Otherwise, why not burn a few people in the street, or—'

Feiffer said reasonably, 'But, Christopher, to terrify them into doing *what?*'

'Into parting with the forty five million dollars!'

Feiffer said, *'What forty five million dollars?'*

'I don't know.'

Auden said, 'I saw that movie. It was called *McQ.*' He looked at O'Yee dismissively, 'It turned out in the end the policeman was the one who did it.' He said with feeling, 'A load of bloody Saturday afternoon *rubbish!*'

There was another movie, a silent epic made in 1921 called *The Villain's Come Uppance.* In it, the big guy sitting at a table in a restaurant making disparaging comments about the poor but honest hardworking tryer, got a plate of noodles in the face for his trouble.

Luckily for Auden, O'Yee, uncharacteristically, seemed to have missed that one.

*

Bell. There was still Bell.

Mrs Bell must have been standing next to him at the phone because Ashwood's voice said more gently than Feiffer would have expected, 'Yes? Jack Ashwood speaking?'

'I'm sorry to bother you at a time like this, Jack. It's Harry Feiffer.' (Ashwood said easily, 'Yes, I know who it is.') 'But I thought if I could have a word to Mrs Bell and try to—'

Ashwood said icily, 'Yes, thank you very much. That's very good of you. I'll pass your sympathies on to Mrs Bell.' He seemed to take his mouth away from the receiver for a moment. Feiffer heard him say something about everything being all right and it was just someone from the

Department. Mrs Bell's voice said very clearly, on the verge of tears, 'It's him, isn't it?' Ashwood said to Feiffer, 'Is there anything else?'

'Yes. I want to try and explain to her that her husband is simply—' Feiffer said awkwardly, 'That there are so many unanswered questions—about the suit and Bell's disappearance in the hotel when the money was burned and—' It was hopeless, 'I just wondered if there was anything she might know that—'

'What would she know?' Feiffer heard Ashwood say as an order, 'You go and rest. I'll talk to him. If you like I can get my wife or one of the neighbours to—' Ashwood said, 'I don't think she's got anything to say to you at all.'

'Look, I'm not in this for the pure pleasure of upsetting bloody widows! There's a lunatic running around loose with a bloody petrol gun looking for God knows what—'

Ashwood said with heavy sarcasm, 'Forty five million dollars. Yeah, I've spoken to the Commander.'

'Yes, forty five million dollars! God knows where that's supposed to be and God knows where the missing firefighting suit he's running around in looking for it in is and God knows where eighty bloody gallons of petrol is – but that's all I've got – and if she can shed any light on it at all – *anything*—'

Ashwood said, ignoring him, 'Her husband was a hero. He was a hero in the war and on a number of occasions – you ask your own bloody Commander – he was a hero in the Fire Service and when he died – *he died trying to save your goddamned people's lives!*'

'He died shutting a door to keep us out! I want to know why!'

Ashwood said tightly, holding back something, 'Every day of his life that man was a hero. Every day of his life—'

'What does that mean?'

'It means something you wouldn't understand! It means that what he did every goddamned waking minute of his life made winning a few medals in bloody Viet Nam nothing! It means—' Ashwood broke off and said softly to Mrs Bell, 'No. It's none of his business.' He seemed unable to drop it, 'It means that the bravest man is the one who's afraid and says nothing! That's what it means!'

'I don't know what you're talking about.' Feiffer said reasonably, 'Listen, tell me where Bell's firefighting suit is and I'll come over there and be the first to—'

'I don't know where it is!'

'Did he at least have one?' Feiffer said, 'Look, I'm prepared to conceive the possibility that he's innocent—for all I know he didn't even have one in his car—'

Ashwood said vehemently, 'Clever bastard time again, is it? Because you've already been told he did, haven't you?'

'Tell me he bloody didn't and so help me I'll believe you! What did you mean when you said that every day of his life he was a hero? When I rang the depot at one stage they told me that he was at the movies. And he wasn't. So where was he?'

'Forget it.' Ashwood said firmly, 'I don't want to say anymore. That man's had enough smears put on his name for one day and I—' Feiffer heard Mrs Bell say in the background, 'For God's sake, Jack—' Ashwood said, 'I'm going to hang up now before I say something, as a cop, I may have cause to regret in bloody Court!'

Mrs Bell's voice said very clearly in the background, 'For God's sake, George didn't need all this hero worship. He was a gentle man, not a—' Mrs Bell's voice said suddenly calmly, 'Jack, if you don't tell him the truth I will—'

Ashwood said into the phone, 'You're upsetting her. You're—'

'What truth? Will someone tell me! *What truth?*' Feiffer said to bring Ashwood's attention back, 'Bell was in the hotel when the money was burned. He must have heard it happen. Why didn't he come up to the foyer immediately and help put it out?'

'Go to hell!'

'What was he afraid of? Was he afraid of something in that hotel?'

Ashwood said as Bell's friend, 'George Bell wasn't afraid of anything.'

Mrs Bell shouted, 'Jack! He wouldn't have wanted it like this!'

Feiffer shouted, 'What? What the bloody hell do you know you're not telling me?'

'Nothing!'

'Listen, Ashwood, people are dead! For all I know that fucking lunatic Bell was the one behind it!'

'You shut up! The only fucking lunatic around here this day is—' Ashwood shouted back at Mrs Bell, 'No, he was my friend!'

'He was my *husband!*'

There was a silence. Then Ashwood drew in a breath. In the background Feiffer could hear what sounded like a woman crying. Ashwood said, 'All right!' He said softly to Feiffer, 'All right. The truth is—' Finding it hard to get it out he drew a breath, 'The truth is—that George Bell was afraid of smoke!' Ashwood said bitterly, 'So now you know. He was afraid of smoke!'

'Are you serious?'

'Yes, I'm bloody serious! God damn it all, you're supposed to be a bloody trained observer! Didn't you see the way he was running in the foyer towards the office? He was red in the face and out of—' Ashwood demanded, 'All right? Happy now? Yes, he was supposed to keep a bloody firefighting suit in his car and no, as a matter of bloody fact, he didn't!' The flood gates released, Ashwood said, 'All right, so he lied by not telling the Brigade and putting people's lives at risk because he wanted to hang onto the one job that meant something to him, but personally, personally I don't give a damn! That man had done his bit and whatever little bloody respite he may have given himself he bloodywell earned a hundred times over!'

'If he didn't keep it in the car then where did he keep it?'

'How the hell should I know? He was never called on to use it so it didn't come up, did it? And I didn't ask.' Ashwood said warningly, 'And don't you think now that if you go running to the Brigade with your little story and those bastards decide to renege on his pension rights that his widow is going to be short dollared, because that man had more friends – real friends – than you could—'

'Are you telling me that he didn't carry the suit with him at all? That if the need arose for a suit he was going to tell the Brigade that he'd left it behind and that—' Feiffer said abruptly, 'Where did he go in the afternoons when he was supposed to be at the movies?'

'He went to the bloody doctor!'

'Why?'

In the background Mrs Bell, sounding composed, said firmly, 'Jack, give me the telephone.' After a moment, she came on the line, 'This is Irene Bell, Mr Feiffer.'

'Mrs Bell, all I'm trying to find out is—'

Mrs Bell said, 'My husband, Mr Feiffer—' She seemed to pause for a moment as Ashwood said something quietly to her in the background and she answered him, brooking no argument, 'No. My husband, Mr Feiffer, didn't carry his suit in the back of his car because, as Jack has just told you, he was afraid that one day he might be called on to use it. And if you've been saying to Jack that my husband noticeably tried to avoid being in the area where fires were actually burning, that's true too.' She paused for a moment, 'Jack thinks that someone stole my husband's suit and that he didn't report it because—' She seemed to direct her voice to Ashwood, 'Because he was George's friend, he may even have thought that George stole it himself.'

Ashwood said, 'No!'

166

Mrs Bell sounded very tired, 'But, George, being George, he didn't. He had emphysema, Mr Feiffer. He contracted it about a year ago and it was getting progressively worse: it's a sort of slow decaying of the lungs and fire or smoke—' Mrs Bell said wistfully, 'That's why he was afraid of smoke and that's why—' She said sadly, 'If he'd worn that suit in a fire it would have killed him. Quite literally he would have been unable to breathe. What we all hoped for was a staff job for him, something in Planning or—' She paused for a moment, 'We all hoped that if he could get through just this year until his promotion was due he might—' She said softly, 'But it wasn't to be.' Mrs Bell said, 'The suit was kept in the back of his car and some nights—some nights he used to wake up—sometimes the thought of— He couldn't breathe, Mr Feiffer and he wouldn't resign because after Viet Nam he felt that he had to pay things back somehow - after he's burned all those - and something to do with a monk in Saigon.' She said quietly, 'Jack knows. But he—' She drew a breath to hold onto her control, 'When that awful, murderous suit was stolen—' Mrs Bell said, 'He was a kind, gentle man, Mr Feiffer, and he was afraid, and the person I knew wasn't the cardboard hero that everyone talked about, it was a—' Mrs Bell said suddenly, 'I stole the suit, Mr Feiffer. My husband's firefighting suit has been hidden in this apartment now for over eight weeks and it couldn't be the one you're looking for because I stole it and hid it—'

Feiffer said quietly, 'And his friends, did they know this?' Ashwood's sudden silence behind her made an answer unnecessary.

'No.' Mrs Bell said, 'No, no one knew it.' She drew a long breath and said softly to Ashwood behind her, 'Jack ...' She said to Feiffer, 'No, Mr Feiffer, they were only his friends.'

'And your husband himself?'

'Yes.' Mrs Bell said, 'Yes.' She sounded somehow

comforted, 'Yes, he knew. I'm sure he did.' She said again, thinking about it, 'Yes ...' Behind her, Ashwood was quiet. Mrs Bell said, 'He was my husband, Mr Feiffer, and I loved him very much indeed and I think he knew I had done it and I think he knew why.' Mrs Bell said softly, 'And I believe that very firmly indeed.'

There was silence. After a moment, Feiffer said softly, 'Yes.' He waited until she hung up then dialled the Commander's number and made a call.

*

10.33 p.m. Making an excuse, The Spaceman disengaged himself from his acquaintance by the car and went across towards the front entrance of the hotel to make ready.

The wind in from the sea had increased in intensity and was blowing papers and torn handbills advertising the Congress up and down the gutters and along the street.

The night was raven dark, the lights from the fire tenders and ambulances illuminating it in blue and yellow flashes like isolated houses and beacons on a secret coastline seen from the sea.

The Spaceman, hurrying a little, like a man late for an appointment, swung his briefcase as he walked.

17

He had missed something. Over and over he had the same
nagging feeling that there was something there directly
under his nose, staring him in the face, and somehow, in
the morass of plot and counterplot, he had missed it.
Feiffer said, 'If it isn't Bell, then who is it? And if it isn't his
suit, then where did it come from?' It was crazy. 'The most
reasonable thing – the most *un*reasonable thing
– is that it was Bell. Unreasonable because he was the
last person we'd suspect of being involved in something
like that and therefore because—' He stopped, 'But real
police work isn't a Sherlock Holmes story. The most
obvious person is usually the one who has done whatever it is—he's the most obvious because—' Feiffer shook
his head, 'No, it's only in the movies that the most unlikely person has done it because the writer can go back
through the script scattering clues in at the appropriate places he hadn't realised were appropriate until
he'd finished the first draft – this whole goddamned
thing doesn't sound real – it sounds like something out
of—'

O'Yee said with satisfaction, 'The movies!'

'But, Christopher, in the movies there's always a mistake
in reality. That's why it is a movie!' Feiffer said, 'That
Agatha Christie one – the famous one – where everyone on
an island gets bumped off one by one until there's no one
left to suspect, that assumes that in real life people would

be fooled by phoney blood and that they wouldn't be able to tell when someone was really dead—'

O'Yee said easily, '*And Then There Was One*. This bastard whoever he is doesn't seem to have made any mistakes. And then, just when we think it's obvious that Bell was—'

Feiffer said, 'If The Spaceman planned all this step by step he shouldn't be thinking about the movies, he should bloodywell be in them!'

Helpfully, Spencer said, 'It's a pity Wong was killed.'

'Is it? I get the feeling that even if we'd beaten him to shit he wouldn't have been able to tell us anything. All Wong seemed concerned about at the end was the fact that The Spaceman set fire to the million dollars. I don't believe all this stuff about Wong wanting bankruptcy. I think Wong was led along on the same series of dance steps as us and that he genuinely believed that The Spaceman was only there to help him in his plans to have the hotel taken over by the Yakuza and himself installed as manager.' Thinking it through, Feiffer said, 'If he had known what The Spaceman's plans were then he would have known who The Spaceman was. Yet when the money went he didn't confront him directly in his civilian role, he barricaded himself in a hotel room with a knife. I think Wong may have sold an idea to someone like the Yakuza and The Spaceman may have sold another built on top of it, and The Spaceman's offer won.'

O'Yee asked slowly, 'Are you saying that there isn't something worth forty five million in that hotel?'

'No, I'm saying there is. Obviously, since The Spaceman burned one million dollars we can assume that what he wants is worth at least more than that. I think the forty five million dollars, so far as Wong was concerned, may have just been a come-on suggested to him by the Yakuza, but I think, so far as The Spaceman is concerned, it really does exist. I think when The Spaceman burned the million Wong may have realised it. And that he wasn't the boss anymore, but just another expendable servant.'

Spencer said, 'Because The Spaceman decided, once The Green Slime didn't turn up, that that part of the plan – the smokescreen – wasn't going to work.'

'I don't know. Maybe. But a smokescreen for what worth forty five million dollars? And if it was Bell who supplied the space suit what would he have got out of it other than maybe a straight rental fee?' Feiffer said, 'But it isn't Bell and, almost as if we were right back at the start, we've got nothing.' He expelled a long sigh and said bitterly, 'Maybe we ought to forget about police work, scribble down the plot and bloodywell sell it to Agatha Christie for her next story.'

O'Yee, his theories being totally ignored, said, 'She's dead.'

Feiffer said in an undertone, 'Lucky old her.' Every way he turned it still came back to Bell's suit. Bell's suit was in a locked briefcase in the bottom of Mrs Bell's cupboard. Feiffer said, glancing at O'Yee, 'Somewhere, just because it *isn't* happening in a movie, there's a mistake. Somewhere, because the scene can't just fade out into black while the audience assumes some minor development takes place, there's an error, something that in the real world can't be assumed. Somewhere, The Spaceman had to walk down a street and do something, or enter a building and arrange some minor point and there he made a—*but what?*'

Auden said, in his own little world, 'One thing I don't like about the movies is where they get the guns from. I saw a movie the other day set in London and the bad guys wanted a few guns so they just turned up. In bloody London these days if you want a gun you have to fill out about five hundred forms and wait for six months.' He saw Spencer about to make some comment on war souvenirs and the underworld market and he, the expert, said quickly, 'No, these were big magnums, see, and nobody has magnums in a war and even if you could steal them—' He noticed a distinct lack of interest in his comments, 'It's like these car chases you see where the car takes off into the air and then hits the ground and keeps running. A real car would be lying about in bits with its suspension shot to shit. Or these ordinary guys in the movies who just happen to know how to hot wire a car or—' closer to home. He gave Spencer a meaningful glare, 'Or know how to bloodywell tell one car from another!'

Spencer, glancing away, shrugged apologetically.

Feiffer said heavily, 'So far as we know the only car The Spaceman has used has probably been his own, no doubt legally registered, taxed, in perfect running order and with probably all four tyres with the perfect legal bloody depth of tread on them—' Feiffer said to clear his mind on Bell for once and for all, 'Look. Bell: what did he do in the hotel? He stopped, right? He grabbed the door. He looked up—'

Auden said, 'He was praying—maybe. He knew he was about to get the chop and—'

Spencer said, '—he closed the door. He—' It got nowhere, 'But it isn't Bell. You spoke to his wife, Harry, and she told you how she—'

Feiffer said abruptly, 'No.' Magnums and cars with strengthened suspensions and ordinary people who— Feiffer said, 'No. She didn't tell me how, but only that—' He saw O'Yee looking at him with a confused look on his face. 'She didn't tell me *how* she had stolen her husband's suit, she just said she had! Auden, you're a bloody genius!' (Auden said, 'Well, yeah—') 'She didn't say she'd taken his suit from the depot or from his car or from—*she simply said that she'd taken it!!*'

In the movies it was more dramatic. O'Yee said, shaking his head, 'No, obviously what she did was go to his car, open it and—'

Feiffer said, 'How?'

'Well with her husband's keys of course. She waited until he'd driven his car home one night and—'

Auden, the persecuted Incredible Hulk of the automobile world, said, 'Like hell he did! I smashed in the window of that bloody car and it was an official Brigade vehicle with a decal on it and everything!'

'So what?' O'Yee looked at Feiffer.

Feiffer said to Auden, 'Tell him.'

Auden said, 'Um—'

Spencer said, 'So if it was an official car he wouldn't have been *allowed* to drive it home. He would have had to have left it at the Depot at the end of his duty.'

'He could have had it during the day. She could have followed him and in the excitement of a fire she could have easily—'

Feiffer said, 'He avoided fires.'

'Then while he was at the doctor's.'

'Sure. He was so terrified of losing his job because he was suffering from emphysema that he took his official, marked car across to the doctor's office and parked it out in plain sight right next to his brass plate, right?' Feiffer said, 'Like hell he did. He probably took the bloody bus!'

'What are you getting at?'

'What I'm getting at is that unless she was a female version of one of Phil's average movie actor joes who just happen to have picked up the technique of picking car locks at high school along with biology and history of Western Europe and bloody domestic science, then if she took the suit from the car she must have had a key!' Feiffer said before O'Yee could protest, 'There are half a dozen police vehicles available for use by the personnel at this Station, Christopher, when was the last time you took a set of their keys home and left them on the hall table?' Feiffer said, 'They're all handed in at the end of duty, signed for by the desk Sergeant and put away in a locked drawer.'

'Then how did she get them?'

Spencer said, 'Not Mrs Bell? You're not saying that Mrs Bell is—'

Feiffer said quietly, 'No, I'm not saying that at all. What I'm saying is that Mrs Bell has her husband's suit all right and that her husband's suit was taken out of his car just the way she says and that the suit The Spaceman wears—'

O'Yee said urgently, 'Yes?'

Feiffer said with a strange smile on his face, 'It's Bell's suit. Mrs Bell, just like her husband, has a friend, and that friend—'

O'Yee said flatly, 'I don't believe it.'

'Don't you? Don't you believe that in the real world, unlike the movies, there's that one little bit of detail that gets skated over because it never shows up on the finished product?' Feiffer said evenly, 'All the big bits we've seen on the silver screen of the Empress of India hotel – the spectacle we've been treated to publicly – have been planned out, worked out, thought through and executed faultlessly because The Spaceman has walked through the motions over and over and had time to *create* the thing. It's his illusion and he was free to vary it as he liked—to kill targets of opportunity and to—*and to make the movie!* But you're right, Phil, the details—the details remain unchanged because they're not part of a movie, they're part of the physical world, they're not part of the illusion at all.' He turned his gaze to Spencer, 'You can do a high speed car chase on film all right and you can have the bad guys all walking around with bloody anti-aircraft cannons if you like, but you can't change the fact that cars won't withstand high speed car chases without being strengthened and that anti-aircraft guns just aren't available!'

Auden said, 'Yeah, you just can't fool an expert with something that's wrong.' He nodded sagely to Feiffer, 'Right, Boss?'

'Right.' Feiffer said, 'Mrs Bell had a friend and her friend, not Mrs Bell herself, was the one who took the firefighting suit. It was her idea all right, but he was the one who actually did it and the chances are, because of the way the whole thing was planned – because of the things we thought about Bell – the motives, the equipment, the opportunity—' Feiffer said, 'That her friend—'

Auden said fiercely to Spencer, 'Right!'

Feiffer said easily, the simplicity of it for the first time since the death of the street sweeper crystal clear and possible, 'Is The Spaceman.' He looked at Auden, 'Isn't he, Phil?'

Auden, astounded, said, 'Yeah. Right.' He looked at Spencer to see if Spencer was nodding. Spencer looked confused. Auden said unconfidently, *'Right!'*

*

On the phone, Feiffer said quickly, 'Mrs Bell, is Superintendent Ashwood still there with you or has he left?'

He had stepped out for a moment.

'I see.' Feiffer drew a breath. Feiffer said slowly, 'Mrs Bell, I wonder if you'd do something for me? I wonder if you'd go into your kitchen, find the strongest, sharpest knife you can lay your hands on and then, when you've got it, come back to the phone so I can ask you to do something rather important with it for me?' Feiffer said quietly and calmly, 'I'd appreciate it very much at this stage if you didn't ask me why.'

Forty five million dollars. He still hadn't the faintest idea where it was or what it was, but by God, thinking it through as he waited, he thought he sure as hell knew who, at least, was trying to steal it.

*

11.25 p.m. The Spaceman, still in his civilian clothes, carrying his briefcase, moved easily through the silent

175

crowds in the hotel foyer and stopped to talk for a few moments to the female night manager at the front desk to ascertain that his timing was right.

It was. The old woman at the grand piano was starting a tune from one of the old English Second World War Blitz movies. It was a pity the crowd were not singing along.

There was a grandfather clock against the far wall of the foyer, near the burned out office and The Spaceman went over to it and examined its face.

The setting on the face read *Silent Chime.*

The Spaceman opened the glass face as if he was checking his watch and moved the little setting lever to *Chime On Hour.*

He smiled to himself.

Just like the Titanic movies and the haunted house movies and all the movies ever seen about natural disasters and the end of the world and death and evil portent the clock would chime in the graveyard hush at exactly—

At exactly midnight.

By the pricking of my thumbs something wicked this way comes ...

The Spaceman ran his eyes across the faces of the hollow-eyed, ashen crowds huddling together in the foyer, saw them only as dead awaiting disposal and burial, and felt for them, in that final moment, only hatred.

11.27 p.m. He moved quickly towards his appointed place to wait out the remaining minutes.

18

If it was a movie then—

Feiffer said quickly over the phone, 'No, I promise you, your husband's out of it. Have you got the knife and the briefcase?'

Mrs Bell said dubiously, 'Yes.' There was a silence.

Feiffer said encouragingly, 'Mrs Bell, the only time your husband actually saw The Spaceman wearing the suit was in the hotel manager's office before he died. Before that, for all he knew, the suit could have been just something someone had hired from a theatrical costumiers or—'

Mrs Bell said quietly, 'And if he did know, or suspect—'

'He didn't. When I rang the Depot he was out and I spoke to—'

Mrs Bell said quietly, 'And if he did know or suspect, he wouldn't have said anything because it would have made him look like a coward for not reporting the theft. Is that what you're saying?'

'No, that isn't what I'm saying. I think The Spaceman thought he would have reported it the moment he saw it, but he relied on the fact that at the first whiff of smoke and fire your husband would have—' Feiffer said quickly, 'Mrs Bell, at the time, I couldn't work out what your husband was doing in the hotel when the money was burned and why he didn't get to the foyer at top speed to help put out the fire. What I think now, in view of what you told me about him, is that your husband, knowing he couldn't help

177

on the spot, was checking that hotel from top to bottom in order to try to prevent the situation even arising. I think he found something and he tried to get everyone out before it happened.'

'What?'

'I don't know.'

Mrs Bell said, 'But nothing did happen, did it? Nothing he could have changed. Jack Ashwood said The Spaceman was in the airconditioning shafts, not in the cellars, and even if George had—'

'No, something else. Something to do with eighty gallons of missing petrol.' Feiffer said hopelessly, 'But I don't know what.' He appealed to her, 'Please. Slide the blade of the knife in under the hinges of the briefcase – don't bother about the locks – and give the knife a hard twist.' If it was a movie then— Feiffer said urgently to the woman's silence, 'Look, if you want to get your husband out of this free and clear, for God's sake put the knife in under the hinges and break the case open!' If it was a movie then— Feiffer said with an effort at reasonableness, 'Mrs Bell, listen, if Jack Ashwood were there then I could—' He glanced at O'Yee watching him and appealed in the silence of the room in an undertone, 'Come on, please!' There was a clear snapping sound on the line and he asked anxiously, 'Have you done it? Is the case open?'

There was a pause and then Mrs Bell, still unconvinced, said evenly, 'It's open.'

'And?'

It was. It was a movie. And the producer had made his one little between-the-scenes mistake in reality. Mrs Bell said quietly, sounding surprised, 'It's empty, Mr Feiffer. There isn't anything in it. No suit, no—' She seemed struck by sudden alarm, 'It's empty! My husband's firefighting suit isn't in it at all!'

'Mrs Bell, I know you don't happen to have the expertise yourself to pick the locks on car doors and to walk away in

178

plain sight with a stolen Brigade briefcase under your arm ...' Feiffer said with an effort at calm, 'So tell me, would you: the briefcase, just who was it who delivered it to you?'

Putting it all together, considering that it had been Bell who had been suspected from the beginning, the name she gave him, in view of its obvious connection with Bell in every way, shouldn't have surprised him at all. Feiffer said, 'Thank you very much.' Forty five million dollars ... Feiffer said for the second time, 'Thank you very much indeed.'

It was exactly 11.35 p.m. For some prophetic reason he looked at the Station clock.

*

Standing at his desk to make his point more histrionically, at the end of his tether, O'Yee said, '*What* forty five million dollars? There isn't any forty five million dollars!' A small part of his anger was guilt at his own mental inefficiency, 'It's all very well talking about forty five million dollars when there is forty five million dollars—*but there isn't!* We don't know any more than when we started! All we've got is another suspect and we – we haven't got any forty five million dollars – and we haven't got any missing eighty gallons of petrol! There isn't anything worth that sort of money—not in the hotel, not in the entire Colony, not in the entire—' O'Yee demanded, 'We know who he is—why not just pick him up and—'

Feiffer said with a snarl, 'And what? Beat it out of him? Beat *what* out of him? Tell me what he's after!'

Spencer, shaking his head, said desperately, 'It has to be something small, or at least portable. It has to be something that he can carry away—'

Auden said, 'Like what? The hotel?'

O'Yee said, 'Sure, the hotel. Of course it's the hotel. He's

179

going to take the hotel away and re-erect it for the Yakuza in down-town Tokyo, but you know what the Japanese are like about miniaturization: they feel it's a bit too much on the bulky side so he's obligingly burning it down piece by piece so he can put it in his goddamned handbag to make it easier to carry!' He snapped at Auden, 'Of course it's not the fucking hotel you stupid cretin! It's something big, worth millions he can—' He stopped himself, 'How the hell can it be big and worth that sort of money if it's small?' He turned his gaze to Feiffer, 'Harry, we've only got the word of The Green Slime that the forty five million dollars even exists—and he had it from Wong who may have got it wrong or simply said it as a come-on. How do we know The Spaceman isn't after something entirely different?'

'We don't. But what else could it be? What else could be worth this sort of slaughter? If it was just, say jewellery in someone's room or in the hotel safe, why not just—' Feiffer said, 'What ever it is—'

Auden said, 'It's invisible, just like the goddamned Volkswagen van!'

Irritated at his own stupidity, O'Yee said, 'What the hell's as big as the goddamned Queen Mary – because that's the only sort of thing worth forty five million anythings – and as small as—so small you could carry it away? And who the hell would buy it?' He thought it through. 'Do you realise that if it's being sold for forty five million as stolen property, on the legitimate market it might be worth at least twice that?' The figures loomed into incomprehensibility, 'The only thing worth ninety or a hundred million is a goddamned—' He stopped, stunned, 'Is a goddamned—is *nothing*! Nothing is worth that sort of money!'

Feiffer said slowly, 'Maybe it doesn't have that sort of worth for what it is but for what it can turn *into*.' He glanced around the room to see if that made sense. It

180

didn't. Feiffer said, 'A piece of technology for an electronic calculator or—'

Auden said evenly, smiling thinly at O'Yee, 'Calculators cost about ten dollars each. At that rate, to break even—'

Feiffer said, 'I mean, a computer or something.' He answered his own question, 'I can't see IBM paying out forty five million dollars for a piece of stolen hardware and spending the rest of eternity fighting court actions for theft and patent infringement by actually using it.' Feiffer conjured up a mental picture of the hotel and tried to visualise where he had stumbled past a solid gold statue in one of the corridors and not noticed, 'Even goddamned gold isn't worth that much – nor heroin – nor—' He looked hard at Spencer for evidence of his expensive education, 'Radium? Maybe, say, a pound of radium—'

Spencer shrugged apologetically.

'Well, yes or no?'

Spencer said, 'There isn't that much radium in the entire world.'

O'Yee said, 'It has to be something *big!* I may be stupid, but I don't believe there's anything in existence worth forty five million bucks that doesn't actually *look* like it's worth forty five million bucks. And if it's worth forty five million bucks, it's *big!*'

Spencer shook his head, 'But it has to be small, Christopher, or he couldn't carry it away.' He suggested, 'A piece of art? But then who'd buy it? Even if you were the sort of mad millionaire who didn't care whether or not it was stolen and you just wanted to gloat over owning it—'

Auden snapped, 'That's just on the movies, that doesn't happen in real life!' He went on before O'Yee could differ, 'And anyway if you paid that sort of money – even if you were a millionaire – you wouldn't have enough left over to buy a goddamned chair to sit on and gloat *in!*' He came up with his own master stroke, 'A new sort of weapon.'

O'Yee said in an undertone, 'Yeah, a stupid-ray. One hit and it turns morons into instant geniuses ...'

The wall clock stood at 11.40. Feiffer, glancing at it, asked curiously, 'But why all the trouble? If as you say, Christopher, it's a movie plot, then which movie exactly is it?' He raised his hand to silence O'Yee before he spoke, 'Yeah, I know, all of them—but still, why all the trouble? Why terrorise an entire community? An entire hotel if—' Feiffer said abruptly, 'It's not the hotel at all. We've been thinking about the hotel as if it was something particular and separate, but, surely, it's the people *in* the hotel.' The thought ran away into nothingness, 'But what have they got worth forty five million dollars? How many people would the hotel hold? Twelve hundred? Even if anyone could get that many people together with one central thought it wouldn't be a hotel, it'd be a bloody Army brigade or something out of *Murder On The Orient Express!*' He became lost in his own confusion. 'How the hell can something take up a lot of space and, at the same time, not take up much at all?' He glanced at Spencer quickly, 'Other than the famous non-appearing Volkswagen van in the carpark?'

Spencer said, 'That was on film. That didn't exist.' He corrected himself, 'Oh, it *had* existed. It existed when he filmed it, but when we saw it—'

O'Yee said bitterly, 'Maybe he's a big movie buff and it's the entire hardware from *Space Wars* and *Close Encounters Of The Third Kind* all thrown in together.' O'Yee said with a curl of his lip, 'The only thing worth anything in the region of forty five million dollars these days is a goddamned free ticket to the—' O'Yee said suddenly, 'The cost of ten minutes of filming one of those movies was about a million dollars—right? That's the amount in the glass case that The Spaceman burned because it was peanuts. If a movie is, say, two hours long, it would have cost to make it—' He tried to work it out mentally, 'Um,

182

one hundred and twenty minutes times...' Deflated, he came up with the total expenditure, 'Only twelve million dollars.'

Auden said with heavy irony, 'Oh, I give that sort of small change to charity collectors all the time.'

'What about four of them?' Spencer said encouragingly, 'That'd be—'

O'Yee finished for him, 'About twenty thousand dollars in exposed film stock and about twenty bucks for the price of admission tickets.' He thumped his hand on his desk, 'And, whatever it is, it doesn't matter to the buyer if it's stolen ...' He appealed to his fist on the desk, 'It's a plot from a movie! I know it's the plot from a movie, but I just can't—' He became desperate to the point of unreality, 'Maybe it's the plot of one of the new movies they're premiering tomorrow night and it's all just one big publicity stunt. The ultimate snuff film: a cast of charred corpses and burning cities.' O'Yee said hopelessly, 'What the hell do I know? I'm not going to get any goddamned movies this week or ever anyway. The best I'm going to be able to do is creep into some flea pit with the rest of the peasants about a year from now and—'

Movies—everything always came back to movies. Something that, in the real world, didn't exist, took up no space— Feiffer said urgently to O'Yee, 'Christopher, how the hell did we come up with the idea that it was all some sort of collage of dozens of movies—all the clichés and expectations from films long dead and gone and—'

Spencer said, looking up, a strange light in his eyes, 'And in the popular consciousness? Because of you, Christopher! Because you've seen all the movies!'

Auden said scathingly, 'Him? Where the hell would he get forty five—'

Feiffer ignored him, 'Or someone like you. Say, like a—'

O'Yee asked, 'A movie producer? The people at the hotel? To do what?'

'To expect something. To expect that even though the hotel was burning that—'

Auden said with heavy sarcasm, 'Yeah, they'd expect that in the end the good guys would catch the villain. I saw those bloody movies too. Before I became a cop I used to think they were true—'

Feiffer said, 'Exactly.'

O'Yee said, 'So what?'

'So they'd do—?' Feiffer said, 'Whatever they were doing previously, i.e. staying at the hotel—which doesn't matter anyway because there aren't any spare rooms anywhere else ... and believe that in the end the good guys would—' What was large as a galaxy and as small as the image of a Volkswagen truck in—? Feiffer said at once, 'That woman Carole, the piano player, told me that the Triads controlled some of the distributors so if you were worried about the safety of your twelve million dollar film—'

O'Yee, far from convinced, said, 'They haven't got distributors. That's why the producers are here for the premieres. If they were worried about the security of their films they'd simply hide them under their beds until—' He asked rhetorically, 'With a Spaceman with a flame gun going around setting things on fire at random? No, they'd put them in the hotel safe because it's fireproof!'

Feiffer said, 'It's the films. He's after the films.'

'But they're not worth anything! They're only prints. A film maker doesn't send his little roll off to Kodak to show on his home movie projector. He's got a master print all right, but the first chance he gets he runs off dozens of prints (a) for later distribution and (b) just in case the master ...'

Feiffer was smiling, O'Yee couldn't understand why. Feiffer said sweetly, 'And, Christopher, if someone like you—or even just someone ordinary, just an ordinary film fan - if someone like that wanted to see a movie and he couldn't or simply didn't want to go to the movie houses to see it—'

O'Yee's face went ashen. 'He'd buy a cassette, authorised if he wanted to wait months or, if he didn't, if he wanted it while it was still fresh, a pirate. A video tape, like—'

Auden, nodding, said 'Like the Volkswagen! Like the Volkswagen that took up a lot of space – that was so big that it – *and at the same* time was so bloody small it didn't exist at all!' He asked O'Yee quickly, reaching for a pad, 'What the hell's a pirate cassette cost? I've seen them on sale in the back streets with the Japanese music cassettes and the—' Auden said in sudden realisation, 'They're Japanese! They're made by the goddamned Yakuza!'

Feiffer nodded. 'Christopher, you must have bought them. What do they cost? About fifty US dollars each? Times what? How many would they sell in Asia alone, in the backstreets and in the thieves' markets and—'

O'Yee said, 'About—' He shrugged, 'About, I don't know— say, a quarter of a million each—' He saw Auden's pencil scratching on the paper, 'Times, say thirty dollars each wholesale is—is ... is about seven and a half million dollars, times ...'

Feiffer asked quickly, 'And how big would one of these film prints be?'

'Well, you'd need to—' O'Yee said, 'Um, a metal transit case carrying say six reels would weigh about sixty pounds. If you had a bag and nobody questioned what you were doing I suppose you could carry away about three if they were all together in one place – in a *safe* – and you had access to something like a hotel porter's luggage trolley—! Um, so the value would be—' He squinted hard to calculate it, 'Say seven and a half million added to what you would probably sell in the States and Australia and – which is, say another six times as many – which is—'

185

Auden, looking up from his pad, said quietly, 'Forty five million American dollars.'

11.43 precisely. The minute hand made a clicking sound.

Nodding, O'Yee said in a whisper, 'Right. To the penny.'

*

On the phone, Ashwood said, 'What? You did what?' There was a silence at the other end of the line and Ashwood said desperately, 'Irene! You did what? You opened it and you told him—' He demanded, 'When? When did he ring?'

'He said it'd clear George for once and for all, Jack! I didn't know what else to do! As soon as I picked it up I remembered thinking that it had felt light and I—' Mrs Bell said to the sudden dial tone in the receiver, 'Jack! Jack! Are you there?'

In the empty apartment, the briefcase lying broken and open on the carpet in front of her, Mrs Bell, calling for she knew not what, shrieked on the edge of sudden prescient hysteria, 'Jack! *I thought getting the briefcase for me was the action of a friend!*'

*

11.57.

There was plenty of time. Spencer, standing by the door, gently shepherding the guests out into the street, said smilingly in English and then Cantonese, 'Don't be alarmed. There's nothing to worry about. We're just clearing the hotel. There's no danger. We're all just going to take a walk down to the end of the street and the firemen there will probably give us all a nice hot cup of tea and we can—' He saw the lady piano player pause by her grand piano and went across still smiling and touched her on the arm, 'It's all right, nothing is going to happen. We know what The Spaceman wants and we're just going to take it out of here so he'll see it go and—' He saw a look of terror start on the woman's face, 'It's not a bomb. Everything's perfectly all right …' The woman swallowed and moved towards the door with him, 'That's fine …' He saw O'Yee and Auden at the front desk talking to the Israeli night manager, 'See, the police are all over the hotel, there's nothing to worry about …' He got the woman to the glass doors and gently propelled her towards the steps, 'That's fine, out you go …'

Carole said, 'I'm not a child, Detective Inspector, and I'd appreciate it if you didn't talk to me as if I was!'

Spencer, not hearing the words, gave her a winning smile.

At the front desk, O'Yee said urgently to the Israeli, 'How many?'

It took slightly more than mass arson to unhinge a Sabra. The girl said, 'Seven or eight, I think. I checked them in and receipted them as exactly what they were: exposed films with the insurance liability just the cost of flying out replacements from the studios. That was their own view—the producers.'

The last of the crowd was going. O'Yee looked around for Feiffer and saw him standing in the blackened doorway of Lam's office, shaking his head. O'Yee said, 'Who's idea was it to put them in the safe in the first place? Was it the man I said?'

'Yes. He was an official—in uniform—' The girl shrugged at a lifetime of conscript Army service— 'Well, I just did what he told me. The producers were all telephoned and told that the safe was fireproof and for the sake of security they were recommended to gather them all together and—' She asked briskly, 'The combination's here. Do you want me to get them out?'

'As soon as everyone's gone. If he is watching the hotel we want him to see us carry them out and—' He wondered why the girl looked at him oddly.

He stopped. He looked up. He closed the door. In the smashed and burned doorway, Feiffer shook his head and said to himself, 'Why? What did he see?' There was nothing. All he would have seen was the foyer. Feiffer stepped back a little into the office and smelled burned wood and scorched plaster. A fine rain of dust came down from the ceiling as he moved. Feiffer said aloud, 'He stopped. He looked up. He—' He craned out the doorway, trying to remember where Bell had stood. Eighty gallons of petrol ... But if Bell had known where it was, why had he given up once he was in Lam's office? That was what he had done, given up. Feiffer said, 'He stopped. He looked up. Then he seemed to somehow give up and then he—' He looked at what was left of the door, 'And then he closed the door and held it shut.'

Against what?

If he had simply moved to one side to save himself then they could have killed The Spaceman and—

Everybody. He had tried to save everybody.

Feiffer said aloud, 'He stopped. He looked up—'

It was almost as if closing the door was enough, that there was nothing more he could have done, no more that was possible to—

To do *what?* To save *who?* And to do it *how?*

There was nothing in the manager's office but The Spaceman and Lam and Wong and, on the other side, in the foyer, just— Both rooms were exactly the same—

He stopped. He looked up. A fireman, he saw something that—

If anyone had hidden the eighty gallons of petrol in the foyer then it was invisible. There was nothing in the foyer that wasn't in the office other than – he looked up – a chandelier and plaster work and different coloured paint and a slightly higher ceiling pocked every six feet with—

Feiffer said suddenly, 'Oh, my God—!' He turned back into the office and peered at the ceiling. It was different. Frozen, Feiffer said in a gasp, 'It couldn't be—!'

At the desk, O'Yee said, 'What do you mean haven't we got him already? Of course we haven't—what makes you think—' He saw the look on the girl's face, 'You said he asked you this afternoon—he's come back and checked, hasn't he!'

'Yes.'

O'Yee said, 'When?' There was a heavy click and then the grandfather clock made a mechanical whirring sound as a precursor to striking the hour. O'Yee, reaching for his gun, said urgently, 'When? When did he check?'

'Just now! He's in here now!'

Feiffer yelled, 'Christopher! The eighty gallons of petrol—my God, it's in the bloody *sprinkler system!*' He saw Ashwood rush in through the front door, gun drawn. Ashwood shouted, 'What the hell's—' then there was a noise from behind Feiffer in the darkened office, and before he could get himself fully out of the way, The Spaceman—Deputy Fire Safety Officer Peter Chang, the man who had all the same opportunities as Bell, Bell's friend and the friend of Bell's wife—looking like something from Hell, appeared in the doorway, pressed the trigger of his flamegun and, sending the gust of roaring, boiling flame along the ceiling like a wave of lava, ignited the sprinklers and, in a storm of falling, searing yellow flame, set the foyer totally and instantly alight from one end to the other.

He had a rolled up asbestos bag in his hands for, first, carrying the plastic explosives for the safe and then, second, for the films he was going to carry away on one of the luggage trolleys by the front desk.

He fired again and blew the twin glass doors out in a shattering explosion that knocked Spencer off his feet and propelled him out into the street in a shower of flying glass and metal.

The Israeli girl was up and onto a smashed and broken window, clambering her legs over the edge. The front desk seemed briefly immune from the fire. She glanced back once, then, as gunshots began to go off in the midst of the inferno as Auden got his magnum out and fired blindly, screwed her courage up, and, shouting something to God in Hebrew, gained His ear, and leapt to safety.

Firemen outside were running. They were trying to bring their foam hoses to bear.

Everywhere she seemed to hear people screaming.

19

Outside in the street, Spencer shouted, 'Get the water hoses on the sides of the building!' The Israeli night manager was half running, half hopping away from a smashed window and he thought to run to help her, saw her miraculously recover from her foot injury and begin fleeing towards the end of the street, and caught hold of a fireman's shoulder and directed the torrent of water from his hose at the blown out front entrance. The jet of water hit the flames with a crack like wood snapping and vapourised into steam.

There were pathways between the maze of flaming sheets of falling petrol. The air was filling with steam and thick cloying smoke from burning chairs and carpets. Something huge fell down from the ceiling somewhere in the midst of the flames and sent showers of sparks and spinning globules of liquid fire into the pathways. Feiffer got to his feet, retched with the thick smoke and then got back down to his knees. A shot went off clearly on the other side of the foyer: Auden.

Feiffer had his own gun in his hand. He saw a movement of white or silver as The Spaceman walked directly into the flames towards the front desk and then he was gone. There was another crash in the midst of the fires as one of the public telephone booths by the entrance to the kitchens burned up its full length and then fell over like a building collapsing into the sea. The heat was intense. Feiffer felt

191

the skin of his face drying and cracking. He tried to see O'Yee—

At the far wall, O'Yee had his back pressed hard against a fire extinguisher. The flames were eating up the ground in front of him like a man painting himself into the corner of a room. He got his hands on the extinguisher and tried to yank it free. The metal was heating up. For a moment he saw Auden by the kitchens down on one knee, the big magnum barrel searching for a target. O'Yee yelled out, 'Phil—' He saw Auden go down.

The foam from the high pressure hoses was smashing its way into the foyer through cracked and splintered windows. There was a terrific bang as a stream hit a section of high impact picture glass and blew it out in razor sharp bullets into the foyer and hit the flames and turned into blinding white steam. The foam cleared another pathway. Feiffer saw the sprinkler nozzles on the ceiling discharging their petrol non stop. He saw Ashwood for a moment shaking his head by the telephone booths, then the man looked around, ducked into one of the booths as a wave of flame overwhelmed him and shut the door. Something hard and sharp drove into Feiffer's leg and he batted at it with his hand to put it out. His clothes were smouldering. He saw Ashwood in the cleared path for a moment, suffocating in the telephone booth, and shouted at him to get out.

The Spaceman was half way across the foyer, walking through the flames, his gun firing without ceasing. He saw a long sofa by a row of burning chairs and paused to squeeze off a flame that set it alight from end to end. Fire and burning bits of the ceiling were falling all around him. With his gloved hand he waved them away as if they were gnats.

He had the rolled asbestos bag in his hand. He held it up in front of him, saw the front desk clearly for a moment in a clearing screen of steam, and ignited it in a single burst. Fire was falling down into the key boxes and wooden pigeon holes. Papers and brochures, slips of tickets and pamphlets, newspapers and magazines were on fire. The luggage trolleys were metal. They were safe. He saw a row of gas lighters in a little recess where cigarettes were sold to the guests and exploded them one by one with a held burst. Something struck a chair near him with terrific force and ripped a long splinter of wood away and he turned and saw Auden on one knee in a ring of fire snap open his big revolver and try to get his fingers to reload the empty chambers. The Spaceman brought his gun to bear but the man was gone in a roaring explosion of steam and foam as the firemen outside got another hose into action. There was another shot from somewhere behind him and The Spaceman, with all the time in the world, turned and began walking towards the source to kill it.

O'Yee screamed, 'Godammit, where are you—!?' He saw The Spaceman moving in the flames, coming towards him, and he fired three times blind into the flames. A jet of fire ten feet from his shoulder caught the thin construction of the wall and blew it apart like a charge. Something struck him hard on the side of the head and he thought, "Oh my God, my hair's on fire!" A rivulet of molten flame devoured the carpet in front of him, struck the wall and set it alight above his head. Ashwood was at the telephone booth, gasping for air. O'Yee started towards him. There was no way to get there. He sensed rather than saw a figure coming towards him and gasped to try to clear his lungs and eyes and aim his gun.

The gun was empty. He thought he fired in the crescendo of sound, but there was no recoil. His eyes were drying out: he couldn't blink to clear them. O'Yee felt another push against his back from the wall and then something burning like glass ripped into his back and he thought, "I've had it. I can't get out." He tried to get his spare cartridges out of the loops on his belt. They were red hot and he ripped the loops free and threw them into the fire, feeling himself toppling. Someone grabbed him by the shoulder, somehow crawling along the ground, and he raised the pistol to bludgeon them, but there was no strength left in his arms.

Feiffer said, 'Christopher—!' He was red in the face, like a man running out of air. O'Yee felt himself dragged across towards the fire and said, 'Harry, it's the wrong way—!' Auden was in plain sight for a moment, trying to get a target for his gun. The flames closed in around him.

Feiffer yelled, 'He's at the front desk—! I can't get across to—' Something made a groaning, wrenching sound in the roar – heard clearly, something above the flames – and Feiffer saw Ashwood trying to make his way out of the telephone booth, stumbling—and yelled, 'The chandelier—!' as the chandelier, freed of its restraining guy ropes, fell through the flames like a space satellite and smashed itself to pieces on the burning carpet. There was a series of explosions as the few remaining bulbs detonated and then a deafening volley of cracks as the glass finials and teardrops splintered in the heat and discharged like bullets.

Feiffer was doing something with the wall, pushing at it. A door came open and there was a room clear of flames and smoke, looking normal, as if nothing was happening. O'Yee tried to say, 'What is it?' and then, with a push that threw him onto his face, Feiffer shoved him into the room and doing something from the outside again on the wall, somehow, miraculously closed the door behind him.

O'Yee couldn't work out where he was. The room was moving. He saw lights and heard sounds, then there was a sudden bump and the doors opened again and he was in the cellars. An elevator— O'Yee said with a strange, grateful look on his face, 'It's an elevator. Harry, that's really clever ... that's ...' Feiffer wasn't in the room with him. O'Yee said, *'Harry—!'* The elevator doors started to close again and O'Yee, a moment before he seemed to turn slowly on an axis and lose consciousness with the smoke in his lungs, said, 'No ... no,' wedged himself across the doorway and as the doors tried to close and the electric cables and wires connecting it to its mechanical brain centre in the shaft burned through, was jammed there, safe.

O'Yee said, 'I've got to go back ...' Just one clean gulp of air ... 'I've got to ...' He couldn't stay awake.

A path cleared in a fountain of steam and foam and Feiffer ran across the burning carpet shouting to Auden not to shoot. A table was ablaze with half a dozen suitcases on top of it, their contents spilling out and catching fire. Feiffer saw Ashwood for a moment, standing in the middle of the room by the chandelier, looking down, then the fire closed in again and something black and big went sky high as something under it exploded in a ball of light and launched it. A chair. It burst its way through the flames, turning over and over and seemed to fall apart in mid air. A jet of fire came out from somewhere like liquid metal and ignited it as it fell, then through the flames there was a bang and the chair seemed to fly apart and take to the air again. For a moment, Feiffer saw something in the air in front of him—a cascade of burning newspapers falling down like confetti. There was a rushing sound and a length of carpet in the direction he was going came to sudden fiery life like a fuse and cut off his path. Feiffer shouted, 'Auden, get the hell out of here!' He thought he heard another gunshot, but it was the kitchen doors exploding open and he saw, in an instant, Auden going with them, the gun still in his hand, the man's mouth open, saying something or cursing at something.

Ashwood? Where the hell was Ashwood?

At the safe, The Spaceman reached into his bag and got out the plastic explosive. The safe had a single combination lock and a keyhole and he rammed the entire package of the stuff into the orifice and around the dial as hard as he could, pulled out a length of time fuse and, pausing only long enough to turn and fire his gun for effect into the centre of the walls of fire raging in the room, jerked the metal match on the fuse and dived for the cover of the desk.

The smoke and flames were closing in on him. By the chandelier, Ashwood, his gun still in its holster, said over and over, 'Oh my God ... Oh my God ...' The fires were eating the ground around him, setting him into the middle of a circle. Ashwood said, 'Oh my God ...' Viet Nam. He saw a Viet Cong in black pyjamas with an AK47 stand up, grinning, and then another. The patrol was mesmerized by them. Charlie was standing up in the jungle, smiling, the assault rifles just coming up slowly as if there was nothing to worry about, as if it was all just some sort of exhibition and the guns were only props and the bullets in them only blanks and—Ashwood screamed, 'George! George, *for God's sake do something!*' The Viet Cong were moving towards him – maybe they hadn't even seen him – the Viet Cong were simply standing up from cover in their black pyjamas with their coal black eyes simply looking at him and the wooden guns and blank cartridges in their guns—Ashwood could smell coldness and death coming up with the stink of rotting jungle leaves and humidity. Ashwood said softly, at his last moment, 'George, is that—' He saw Feiffer in an instant, in the midst of the howling fires and shrieked, 'Feiffer, *help me!*'

In the kitchens, Auden said over and over, '*Shit!*' He was lying full length on the tiles, coldness everywhere on his face ... Something was broken in his shoulder and he couldn't reach the gun. His eyes focussed on something big and silver – the cooking ranges along the wall – and he thought ... There were yellow propane gas bottles everywhere in the room. The sprinklers. He twisted to look at them. They were off, maybe even filled with water. The door behind him was making breaking, warping sounds and there was a far off roaring like a ship's engines deep in the hull of … Feiffer's voice seemed to say to him from a long way off, 'You're a genius, Phil!' and Auden tried to shake his head clear, said in a whisper, 'Yeah? I don't even know where I am …' He knew he had to go somewhere, get back to somewhere. He tried to reach for the gun with his good hand, found the butt was hot, and fighting unconsciousness and the aching pain in his shoulder, grasped it and turned himself like a worm to begin crawling back into the flames. The kitchen door seemed to be smoking and bulging like an iron plate under great pressure. His mind wandering, Auden looked for the rivets. Auden said, 'The Titanic—I'm on the—' The roaring of the ship's engines became louder and louder as if something was broken in them and Auden, raving, said with a smile on his face at one of O'Yee's jokes, 'This is the Captain, folks. There'll be a slight delay while The Titanic stops to take on ice.' Auden said, 'No! That isn't—' Bloody shit—Volkswagen vans that didn't exist—sci fi movies—Spacemen, flying saucers—Auden said desperately, 'They didn't have flying saucers when the Titanic went down!' He moved and his shoulder punished him with a paroxysm of pain that curled him up on the tiles like a foetus. Auden, his hand on the butt of the gun, ordered himself, 'No! Do it! Do it!'

In the street Spencer shrieked, 'I don't know where they are!' The firemen at the hoses were protesting. 'Pour it in everywhere!' The second floor of the hotel was smouldering fast and the firemen turned their jets onto the walls to hose them down. Spencer shrieked, 'Into the foyer! They're in the foyer! Put the water into the foyer!' No one seemed to be taking any notice of him and he grabbed the nearest fireman by the shoulder and span him and his hose towards the blown out doors in the foyer, 'Put the flames out in there!' The fireman pulled back. Spencer shouted, 'My friends are in there!' Tears were running down his face. Someone touched him on the shoulder gently to help him away – a fireman – and Spencer yelled at him in hopeless, desperate appeal, 'Please, can't you let the hotel burn and save my friends?'

The piano. The goddamned piano. In the centre of the room, facing the office, the grand piano was the only thing not on fire. Flames were running off its impervious surface like water as the fire temporarily failed to break into the twenty coats of best quality varnish on its highly polished wood. The lid was down. In the heat the metal strings were breaking and pinging. Feiffer got down behind it and snapped the catch on the lid to get it up. Flames licked at the keys and then finding the ivory uninflammable, cascaded down like a shower on the carpet. There was a roar of fire as The Spaceman saw the piano lid go up like a shield and the flames struck hard, melted their way through the varnish and set the lid on fire.

Feiffer was pushing, shoving the enormous thing towards him like a battering ram. The Spaceman's face plate was fogging up with his own laboured breathing. The fuse was burning. He saw a whisp of white smoke. The piano was coming closer and The Spaceman had an image of a revolver and got to his feet to face it. The piano was coming towards him. Feiffer was behind it. Taking aim, The Spaceman turned the nozzle of his petrol gun directly onto the instrument through the flames and set off a ricochetting showering inferno that set it completely alight and disintegrated it. The fuse had only a few seconds to burn. The Spaceman looked through the flames for Feiffer. The man had gone. If he had been near the piano— He saw a shadow move along one of the paths between the flames and then a voice called out, 'George—help me!' Ashwood. The Spaceman turned his head to locate him. The coward Ashwood. The Spaceman saw him and got him clearly chest-on in his sights. The nozzle of the gun was dribbling burning petrol. He saw the shadow in the path move, coming closer. The fuse had only a—

The explosion at the safe came prematurely in a sudden all-enveloping cataclysm, devouring the air in a monstrous blast of raging wind. All the fires went out. The Spaceman saw the safe door open and hanging on its hinges, the films blown out and strewn loose from their cans on the floor. He looked up and saw Feiffer vault over the front desk, soaked in petrol. The petrol was falling unlit from the sprinklers like rain. The Spaceman turned to get his gun. He thought of the films and— Someone knocked him to the ground and he saw Feiffer dive for the safe and grab at the films. The films were all loose and—

The Spaceman raised his gun. Feiffer had the films hard against his chest and was coming towards him. The petrol was falling like a torrent from the ceiling.

The Spaceman yelled behind his helmet, 'No! You'll burn the films!' He heard the petrol falling in an unstoppable hissing and then there was a bang as, far across the room, Auden got the kitchen doors open and stood there swaying with the magnum held in two hands, searching for a target.

Auden shouted, 'Where is he?' He saw Ashwood mute and useless in the centre of the room, his mouth dribbling saliva in fear and he hobbled as fast as he could towards him as O'Yee appeared at the top of the emergency stairs from the cellar and shouted, 'Phil!'

Feiffer shouted, 'Don't shoot! I'm covered in petrol!' He saw The Spaceman hesitate, 'Fire that flame gun and you'll burn everything you've worked for!' The petrol was falling like rain, soaking through into his clothes and feeling like ice on his hands. It was forming puddles where he stood. Feiffer yelled, 'You can't fire that gun because you'll—'

O'Yee yelled at Auden, 'Shoot him!'

'I can't!' Auden saw Spencer race in through the

blackened and smashed front entrance with his revolver in his hand and yelled, 'Bill, the place is full of petrol!'

Behind his face plate, The Spaceman's eyes were staring. He saw the films, the dreams ... His gun would turn them to ashes. He raised the gun and saw Auden weaving to get a killing shot in. Ashwood. Ashwood was wandering aimlessly in the room blocking his fire.

Spencer yelled, 'Phil, the muzzle flash! It'll light the petrol—!'

The window the Israeli had gone out was a few feet from The Spaceman. If he could get out— Feiffer felt the petrol on his face, in his eyes. The films were still in his hands. For a brief second, he saw something seeping from the end of The Spaceman's gun. The safe door was swinging wide on its hinges. Feiffer yelled, 'Don't let him get out!' The Spaceman was going for the window—

Auden and Spencer yelled simultaneously, 'I can't! The petrol!'

Feiffer saw the open safe. There was no sprinkler system in there. Stepping back, he got behind the safe door. The Spaceman was making for the window, the petrol falling everywhere. Feiffer yelled, 'For the love of God, don't let him get out onto the street!' He yelled to Spencer, 'Bill, get out! Auden! Shoot him as soon as Spencer's—'

The kitchen door was swinging. Auden got back behind it. There was a wet towel lying on a table. He grabbed at it, thought quickly, and wrapped it around the muzzle of his magnum. Auden came back into the room and yelled, 'It won't flash! I promise you, it won't—!' He seemed to be hesitating and hesitating. He called out in appeal to Spencer, 'Bill, I'm not sure I can—'

Spencer yelled, 'You're not colour blind! You're fine!' He saw Auden's face, *'Auden, you're a bloody genius!'*

The Spaceman was at the window, reaching up.

O'Yee shouted, *'Shoot him!'*

The single, muffled shot from Auden's gun, striking The

Spaceman exactly in the centre of the back and killing him instantly, pole-axed him where he stood.

For a long moment, his hand seemed to stay on the trigger of the petrol gun, moving spasmodically, and then, as the smoke and the stench in the poisonous room began to clear through the open doors and windows, his hand seemed to relax, the gun made a single clicking sound, and then was still.

The petrol stopped falling from the ceiling and, briefly, there was an utter silence.

Feiffer put the films down carefully on the floor of the safe, his hands shaking. Spencer and O'Yee were standing at the entrance to the safe with fire extinguishers in their hands. Auden reached into his inside coat pocket with a groan of pain and, for an awful moment, Feiffer thought he was going to offer him a lighted cigarette to take away the smell of the petrol on his clothes.

Auden said, 'Here.' It was a clean white handkerchief. Auden said thoughtfully, 'You can use it to wipe your face and hands.' He seemed very happy about something and as Feiffer took the handkerchief and looked into his face he felt he could have—

Feiffer said, 'Auden, you're a bloody—*genius!*'

It was Auden's finest hour. Auden said with a flick of his hand that almost doubled him up with pain, 'Well, thanks, Boss.' He looked at O'Yee. Auden said magnanimously, 'Well, I suppose in this business one of us has to be, doesn't he?'

He turned to Spencer and asked in sudden concern, *'What the hell are you looking at me like that for?'*

*

From the street, Carole could see the iron frame of her grand piano lying in the centre of the burned out foyer, not a single piece of varnished wood intact, not a single yellowed ivory key in place, not a solitary metal string or section of string untwisted, unbroken or unruined.

She was weeping with happiness.

She had nothing to give to show her gratitude, no money or young woman's kiss or—

All she had in her bag were a dozen or so complimentary tickets to the premieres producers had given her at the piano when they heard she herself had once been in the business.

Stupid things to offer grown men.

She saw the Eurasian policeman come out of the entrance to talk to one of the firemen about something and she thought that maybe ...

She went up to O'Yee and, cautiously offering the tickets, wondered if he might accept—

It wasn't a bribe or anything. It was just—

Old woman, nothing. He took her in his arms and kissed her as if she was young, fresh and, like the Carole Lombard she had been called after, joyous, free, and, above all, beautiful again.

*

12.57 a.m. The wind from the sea had dropped, and outside the night was warm and balmy as the firemen moved in to clean up.